The Disappearance of Ichabod Crane

The DISAPPEARANCE OF
ICHABOD CRANE
A Play in Five Acts

By ANDREW WINKEL

Includes the original classic
The Legend of Sleepy Hollow by Washington Irving

HIEROPHANTASM

CLIFTON, ILLINOIS

HIEROPHANTASM

P. O. Box 792
Clifton, IL 60927
hierophantasm.com

The Disappearance of Ichabod Crane: A Play in Five Acts
Copyright © 2011 by Andrew Winkel

Performance inquiries should be addressed to the publisher.

Web addresses included within this work were valid at the time of composition; however the content available at any referenced web address is the responsibility of the content creator, not the author or publisher.

ISBN 978-0-9837905-0-1
Printed in the United States of America

TABLE OF CONTENTS

INTRODUCTION

The Bourbonnais Township Park District in Bradley and Bourbonnais, Illinois, holds its annual "Night at Sleepy Hollow" in October. The mainstay of this event is the recreation of Washington Irving's classic story, *The Legend of Sleepy Hollow*. The original script for this program was designed as a narrative read by costumed actors recounting events from Irving's story. The actors led the audience from bonfire to bonfire, until, at the conclusion of the tale, the crowd raced across a small footbridge while the Headless Horseman appeared astride a horse, chasing them. The crowd was encouraged to "duck" to save themselves as they fled to safety.

I wrote *The Disappearance of Ichabod Crane* in 2005 as a replacement for that original script. As I approached the project I knew that I wanted to expand on the interactivity of the crowd from the original Sleepy Hollow experience; it was important to me that the audience feel the Horseman's chase—not as bystanders—but as characters in the story's action. Through this device, the crowd would literally be actors on the stage of events, immersed in the story, and invested as participants in the final climactic chase of the Horseman. To accomplish this I imagined the audience as a group of concerned locals who had gathered to retrace Ichabod Crane's steps, trying to discover what had happened to him.

After seeing the play *A Year With Frog and Toad* in December of 2004, I was intrigued with the concept of juxtaposition in a play. During the play, Frog tells Toad a scary story about nearly being eaten by the Large and Terrible Frog. While Frog tells Toad the story at one side of the stage, the events of the story are dramatized by the remaining actors at another spot on the stage: one actor is the young Frog, two others are Frog's parents. These two settings played off one another, with characters finishing lines between the two, or yelling at the

1

same time. It worked seamlessly. I wanted to use this device in *The Disappearance of Ichabod Crane*. For this play, I began with the premise that the school kids would wonder about what had happened to their school-master as they came to school the day after Ichabod meets the Headless Horseman. Since it would be impossible to spend the entire play talking about Ichabod without seeing Ichabod, I imagined juxtaposing events from the present (the main characters along with the audience as they search for Ichabod) with events in the past (Irving's characters recounting events from *The Legend of Sleepy Hollow*). This enabled viewers to see and interact with Ichabod and other characters from the story while searching out what had happened to the hapless school-master. Perhaps I was successful in this regard; perhaps not.

I also needed to limit the number of actors used for the performance to try and keep costs down. Plus the audience needed to be moved through the performance, with as many as three to four groups viewing scenes concurrently. I used the original concept of the bonfires, and created a set of four actors who would lead the group from bonfire to bonfire. The goal was to have multiple troupes of main characters leading multiple crowds past multiple bonfires where they would encounter the same fixed actors who would remain at each bonfire. Although this worked logistically, it did not work mathematically. The four main characters could lead three groups simultaneously resulting in twelve actors per night for just four roles. Add the players who remain at each of the bonfires and the script, as written, results in a total cast of eighteen, and that doesn't count the horse! The park district chose to merge two of the main characters, Piper and Mary as one method of controlling costs.

Another factor was time. The performance time for this script was too long for the volume of people attending the nightly performances. What was originally a thirty-six page script was decapitated (or perhaps it would be better to imagine that only the head remains while the body was lost) to about twelve pages. Without Mary and Piper, the bulk of Act One was discarded with the remainder merged into Act Two. Van Ripper's over-long explanation was truncated to a few short paragraphs. Each campfire needed to last only ten minutes, so the acts were shortened accordingly.

In terms of substance, the play succeeds in following *The Legend of Sleepy Hollow* with only minor alterations or embellishments except for one major contradiction: during Act II, Hans Van Ripper laments for his lost horse, Gunpowder; he explains that his horse has not returned, and will not likely return. This is inconsistent with Irving, who writes that Gunpowder showed up the next morning, "soberly cropping the grass at his master's gate." I can no longer recollect whether this deviation from the original story was intentional or accidental. I have left this discrepancy as it was written in the script rather than make the substantial alterations that would be required for the script to match Irving's story.

The original script was revised to fit the format of this edition. During reformatting, some of the original lines and stage directions were moved or revised for clarity. Otherwise, the script remains as it was written in 2005.

Although the Bourbonnais Township Park District has performed the abridged and adapted version of this script since 2006, fully two-thirds of *The Disappearance of Ichabod Crane* has never been publicly seen or read. This edition gives readers an opportunity, for the first time, to read the complete script as it was first envisioned, and in the same slim volume, compare the play against Irving's timeless story.

Andrew Winkel
Clifton, Illinois
June 30, 2011

DRAMATIS PERSONAE

	I	II	III	IV	V

Tom
  Schoolboy who wishes to find what has happened to his school-master. About fifteen.
  X X X X X

Mary
  Schoolgirl who accompanies Tom. About fifteen.
  X X X X X

Piper
  Tom's best friend. About fifteen.
  X X X X X

Ichabod *Crane*
  School-master who has mysteriously disappeared.
  X X X X

Servant
  Baltus Van Tassel's servant.
  X

Hans Van Ripper
  Elderly man who befriends Ichabod.
  X

Baltus Van Tassel
  Wealthy landowner.
  X

Katrina Van Tassel
  Daughter of Baltus; an eligible maiden.
  X

Abraham Van Brunt (*Brom* Bones)
  Local bully and trickster.
  X

The Headless *Horseman*
  Legendary ghost of Sleepy Hollow.
  X

Crowd
  Those locals who have gathered at the urgings of Tom and the other children, and accompany them through the acts.
  X X X X X

4

PROP LIST

Description	Act
School desk positioned in the past	I
Period music for dance	III
Pocket watch for Ichabod Crane	III
Three logs for Tom, Mary, and Piper to sit on	IV
Bridge over gully or creek	V
Pie pumpkins lining the bridge or near the bridge	V
Cavalry sword	V
Horseman costume and black horse	V

AUTHOR'S NOTE:

Character lines are divided into two timeframes: PRESENT and PAST. PRESENT is assumed to be the here and now; that is, the moment in which the play is taking place. No special changes should be made for lines delivered in PRESENT. PAST is assumed to be memories or recollections of characters within the play, and as such, is separated from PRESENT in some slight but obvious way. Characters delivering lines from PAST should be offset, whether behind, or beside the characters who continue observing events from PRESENT.

ACT ONE

(The fire in the first circle is burning. CROWD has gathered, awaiting the players. Enter TOM, MARY, and PIPER.)

TOM:

I don't understand why so few townspeople have come to help. There should be more to find a man lost in these dark woods. All of Sleepy Hollow and Tarrytown should be here right now!

MARY:

Tom, it's not as though everybody liked Master Crane, you know. He was a strange bird.

TOM:

That doesn't mean he deserves to be forgotten. Or left out there-

    Motions to the woods.

I mean, he could have been thrown from the horse. He could have been knocked unconscious. He could be out there with a broken leg. Right now he could be dragging himself through the thorns, exhausted and near death. He could-

PIPER:

Have met up with the Headless Horseman.

    Silence as the players look at one another.

TOM:

Piper, that's just fairy story stuff. Not real. Who really believes those old tales, anyway?

PIPER:

I do.

6

TOM *rolls his eyes, looks doubtfully at* MARY.

MARY:

I do, too.

TOM *puffs, exasperated.*

PIPER:

It's just that you haven't lived around here long enough, Tom. Yeah, I know that two years seems like a lifetime, but there's more to Sleepy Hollow than the woods and the old farmers' barns along the roadways. There's more than the Old Dutch Church. There's something under the surface, if you catch my meaning. Something out of sight. You get to feeling it on chill October nights. You get to feeling it in the dark- ness, and that's when you find yourself glad of being in Church on Sunday mornings.

MARY:

You want to know why there aren't more people here right now trying to find Master Crane? Because Sleepy Hollow folk know that they have no place out in these woods after dark. They've known since settling in this valley, and hearing the uncanny tales of the Indians who dwelt here before.

TOM:

Then why are you here?

MARY:

Because you are. I figure if anybody can find our school- master it'll be you.

TOM:

And Piper? Why are you here?

PIPER:

I keep asking myself that. In fact, I was just thinking I need to get some sleep. In case we have school tomorrow. You know, if Master Crane shows up before tomorrow morning? I can't believe I told my mother that I'd be staying at your house tonight!

TOM:

I'm not asking you to walk alone through the woods at midnight. Let's just follow Master Crane's trail for a bit. See where he went, where he was going. See if we can't figure out what happened to him. We owe it to him.

PIPER:

I don't owe him. I think I've got scars on my knuckles from Master Crane.

TOM:

Well, you can write now, can't you?

PIPER:

Some folks would call it writing, I guess. But my knuckles don't hurt any less.

TOM:

The last time I saw him was yesterday, when he let us out of school early.

> PIPER *moves to the desk positioned in the* PAST *during this line.*

PIPER:

That's right. I was working my multiplication tables. Master Crane was walking by my desk.

> PIPER *sits. Enter* CRANE *with a switch in hand, looking back and forth as though at students seated and working.*

PIPER:

Master Crane said-

PIPER *and* CRANE *simultaneously:*

No, No, No, Piper!

CRANE:

CRANE'S *voice should be reedy, pompous, and exasperated.*

How many times do I have to remind you that three by four equals twelve?

PIPER:

I felt sure I was about to get my knuckles rapped when that servant of the Van Tassel's knocked upon the schoolhouse door.

Enter SERVANT. SERVANT *pantomimes knocking as* PIPER *relates his story.*

CRANE:

Now who could that be? Piper, twelve!

Points severely at PIPER *before moving to the imaginary door of the schoolhouse and answering it.*

Yes?

SERVANT:

Bowing.

Please, forgive my intrusion, Mister Ichabod Crane.

CRANE:

Of course, of course. You are?

SERVANT:

Baltus Van Tassel's man, come on an important errand.

CRANE:

Baltus Van Tassel, why, that's Katrina's father!

SERVANT:

The same, sir. My master requests that you honor his Autumn Festival this night with your presence. You are invited to the house at half past six this evening.

CRANE:

Indeed? Indeed. And it's been quite a long period of time since I last had the pleasure of instructing dear Katrina in singing. She will be there, I presume.

SERVANT:

Of course, sir.

CRANE:

Tell your master I will most assuredly be present tonight, and look forward to the occasion with greatest eagerness.

> *The two bow slightly to each other.* SERVANT *departs.* CRANE *turns and swings his switch triumphantly.*

CRANE:

> *There is a daydreaming quality to the reedy voice that was not present before; an almost sing-song distraction.*

You may all go. All of you...go and be off now.

> CRANE *shoos the imaginary children away.*

Twelve, Piper! Remember twelve!

> CRANE *exits.* PIPER *gets up and moves quickly back to his friends in* PRESENT.

PIPER:

And I sure didn't stay any longer.

MARY:

I saw him briefly last evening. He rode past my house on that flea-bitten horse of old Van Ripper's. He must have borrowed it to attend the party.

TOM:

Van Ripper's horse, you say? Seems we should ask the old man what happened. Come, everyone, let's visit Mister Van Ripper. It's not far.

TOM, MARY, *and* PIPER *lead* CROWD *to the next fire.*

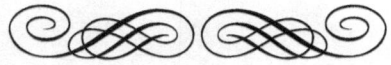

ACT TWO

> TOM, MARY, *and* PIPER *enter the circle of the second fire,*
> *leading* CROWD.

TOM:

Do you think he's home?

PIPER:

Of course he's home. He's got sense, which is more than I can
say for any of us!

MARY:

Here he comes. What luck!

> *Enter* HANS.

TOM:

Sir! Mister Van Ripper! Can we have a word with you, please?

MARY:

Regarding our school-master, Ichabod Crane.

HANS:

You seek a man who cannot be found without losing yourselves.

> *Long pause as* TOM, MARY, *and* PIPER *look at one another.*

PIPER:

Uh, thank you, sir. Tom, Mary, isn't it time we went home?

TOM:

> *To* PIPER.

Not so fast!

> *To* HANS.

Sir? May I ask what you mean?

HANS:

It's a thing you get to knowin' as the years pass. A feeling in the air. You feel it tonight? Look around you at the forest swayin'. Alive, I say. I've lived in these woods since I was your age. A man gets to knowin' things when he puts down roots and I know that these woods are alive. But your school-master, for all his book learnin', wasn't one to listen to advice. I told him! I warned him! And now I've lost poor Gunpowder, the pride of my youth.

PIPER:

Aside.

Gunpowder must have been one old horse!

HANS:

Your school-master came to see me yesterday afternoon. He knocked on the door as polite as you please.

CRANE *enters in the* PAST, *pantomimes knocking on the door, and waiting.* HANS *moves to* CRANE *and opens the imaginary door.*

When I answered it, he said-

HANS *and* CRANE *simultaneously:*

May I come in?

HANS:

Ichabod Crane! To what do I owe the pleasure of your company?

CRANE:

Company?

HANS:

To PRESENT.

He spoke as though his bookish brain had broken. I had a mind that the man had gone queer in the head even then. I should have known no good would come of this!

To CRANE.

Ichabod, I thought you've been staying with the Irvings. Doesn't Mrs. Irving make a spectacular pumpkin pie?

To PRESENT.

You understand, Ichabod Crane's mind is most thoroughly connected to his stomach. If any subject is likely to uncloud his head, it's the subject of his digestion. Yet, oddly enough, he did not swallow the bait.

CRANE:

Pies, of course, pumpkin pie. Exquisite. And yet the Autumn Festival at the Van Tassel's—Ah, *she* is exquisite. I simply must, that is, I must simply...Say, my good sir, of what were we speaking?

HANS:

I believe we were simply exchanging pleasantries before you came to the point of explaining your business in visiting me.

CRANE:

Ah, that. I admit I came to ask a favor.

HANS:

A favor of an old man? How may I help you if not with the wisdom of my years?

CRANE:

Sir, 'tis with pride that I remind you that I am a school-master. A noble profession to share the gifts of knowledge with the youth, and yet never has it been rewarded with wealth. Wise though I be, I lack. Tonight I have been invited to the Van Tassel's Autumn Festival, and I lack the proper carriage.

HANS:

Carriage? You know I don't have a carriage.

CRANE:

Yes. No. I mean, sir, my inquiry regards your horse, Gunpowder. I wondered if you would permit me to ride the steed to the festivities tonight?

HANS:

You want to borrow Gunpowder? Well why didn't you just say so in the first place? I can saddle up my best Sunday saddle, and you can ride in style.

CRANE:

To himself.

Style? Style captures the eye of a lady, yes?

HANS:

To PRESENT.

He kept on talking to himself most irregularly. Peculiar, I thought. It was only later, after he left, that I began to have the fear.

TOM:

Fear, sir?

HANS:

I feared that your school-master had been bewitched. His behavin' brought to mind stories of devils taking over the body of a man, causing him to behave most unnatural-like. But I shouldn't be telling you this!

TOM:

No, sir, really, it may help us to find him.

HANS:

He is gone, children, and not you, nor I, nor any man alive will return him to the fields we know.

Shakes head. Returns to PAST.

Master Crane, let's just get ol' Gunpowder ready for you. But before you go, I must be warnin' you. It's for your own good, of course, you being from Connecticut and not rightly a Sleepy Hollow boy yourself.

CRANE:

Of course. I am intent on keeping your advice.

HANS:

Watch your time. In my years I've seen my share of mysteries in these woods. And I am telling you now that there's forces in this world that dwell in Sleepy Hollow at night. They leave the daytime to us, and keep the night for themselves. The witching hour, Ichabod! Midnight! Honor that curfew and be home before. It is not simply for your rest that I recommend it–It's for your life.

CRANE:

Of course, as you say. As you say.

HANS:

You do know of the Headless Horseman, do you not?

CRANE:

Hm?

HANS:

'Tis he who rides upon a great black horse along the Church Road through Sleepy Hollow. Each night he leaves the grave yard to search for his own head, and that failing, to find the head of any living, breathing mortal to wear for a time.

CRANE:

A fearsome sounding soul he seems. But you spoke of a Sunday saddle. Does that mean I can use it to ride tonight?

HANS:

I did mean such.

CRANE:

Then I shall be the image of a proper gentleman! I shall make an impression tonight. I shall! Let us ready the steed.

HANS:

To PRESENT.

It took only moments to get my best saddle on Gunpowder. And to think it would be the last time I should see the old girl. And to know that her fate was such...I can't bear to think it. I raised her from birth, you understand. The pride of my youth.

But I warned him! Again, I said-

Returns to PAST.

Ichabod, remember the time! Do not be out after the witching hour. The woods do not favor men during the depths of night. Many have been lost and never found. Sleepy Hollow folks know to stay indoors beside a fire when the sun sets. Don't forget!

CRANE:

With much thanks, my good fellow, I will ride to my destiny!

Exit CRANE. HANS *returns to* PRESENT.

HANS:

I did not know the destiny of which he spoke, but I know now that I shall never see Gunpowder again. And after I warned him!

TOM:

Sir, Master Crane could still be out there! Gunpowder could still be out there with him!

HANS:

No, son. She'd be home now. A horse knows where home is. Gunpowder's as Sleepy Hollow as I am. She was my best horse. Raised her from birth, I did...

> PIPER *mouths the following line to the crowd along with* HANS.

The pride of my youth.

TOM:

But why didn't you seek him in the woods during the day?

HANS:

If the Horseman got him, I'll not find him.

TOM:

> *Delivers line to himself in exasperation.*

Why does everyone believe this Headless Horseman is the cause of Master Crane's disappearance?

HANS:

You're not Sleepy Hollow bred, are you?

TOM:

> *Shakes his head.*

No, sir. My family moved to Sleepy Hollow about two years back.

HANS:

It shows. You don't have the look of a boy who's lived with spirits and haunts his entire life.

MARY:

The Horseman has always haunted these woods. Ever since-

HANS:

The Revolution! And a sad tale, it is. A story of war, and of death. My father told me the tale; he was there, you see, when the Horseman fell.

PIPER:

What happened?

HANS:

Like many around here, my father had joined the militia to fight the Loyalists. He fought in a few battles, but the most important battle took place here at his home. You see, the British had brought in mercenaries to aid their weary forces, but more importantly, to do their dirty work. They needed hired hands to burn barns, steal horses, and wreak havoc. They didn't want red coats behaving less than chivalrously, and so mercenary troupes pillaged the colonies, leaving swaths of destruction and despair in their wake.

The Headless Horseman of Sleepy Hollow was once the leader of a troupe of Hessian mercenaries, the most villainous and dangerous of all the mercenaries that the British set upon our coasts. Many a widow and fatherless child owed their sadness to his Hessian troupe.

Finally the Sleepy Hollow militia engaged the Hessian troupe near the Old Dutch Church. Surrounded, outnumbered, with their numbers quickly whittled down by the sharp-eyed Sleepy Hollow men like my father, and by the thunderous report of the cannon fire, there was to be no escape for those murderous thugs.

The Mad Hessian, for that's what some call him, led his men in charge after charge against musket and cannon shot. Any normal man would have surrendered, or lain down until the gunfire stopped, or even tried to run straight off. But not this man. He fought until no one else remained of his mercenary band. He alone was horsed and whole, and indeed my father and his fellows thought perhaps their musket balls were bouncing from him like peas.

Captain Van Brunt looked out over the smoke of the cannons and muskets and saw the great black stallion, its eyes aglow, and believed he was staring straight at a demon of the night. All firing ceased as the lone Hessian charged the line. Just one rider against a whole assembled group of militiamen! But what a rider! It looked as though the line would break, and both horse and man would fly through!

But the stern voice of the Captain brought sense back to the men. "Hold your places!" he spoke calmly. More calmly than he felt, I am sure. Although fearful, the men stayed. And they raised weapons. And as though guided by a mutual force, all canons and musketry discharged in a single volley that so shook the earth and heavens that Father said the sky began immediately to rain. The smoke cleared, quenched by the sudden misty shower. There, on the silent field of battle, lay both the horse and his rider, unmarked and unscathed except the rider no longer bore his head upon his shoulders.

Our boys gave those villains a better burial then they deserved. Afterward no one could quite agree which grave belonged to the Horseman, or if indeed he had been among the bodies buried.

Nightly his spirit rides out from the Old Dutch Church Cemetery, a headless figure astride his great black steed. No one can know why he rides, but most folks believe he's searching for his lost head, and won't rest until he finds it. He may take the head off any unwary traveler he meets along the road, to wear for a time, using it to better search for his own head. Or he may just hunt the living out of spite, that others may share in his decapitation. Either way, no mortal is safe at night with the Horseman about, and your School-master is, I fear, but the latest of the many who the Horseman has met upon the Old Church Road.

Now children, it's late, and I don't aim to see any more Sleepy Hollow families crying in the morning. You children need to be back at home safe in your beds aside a fire. Now, go. Go and get yourselves home right away! Don't you stand here asking me questions and ignoring my advice. Get home before it's too late for you, too!

Exit HANS.

MARY:

What now, Tom?

PIPER:

We go home. That's what old man Van Ripper said. We should heed his advice.

TOM:

You respect your elders?

PIPER:

Well, when they know what they're talking about I do. Might as well just head back-

TOM:

Piper, we're not going home yet. Van Ripper is a superstitious old man. You'll see before we're through. There's nothing to this but a misunderstanding.

MARY:

There's more to this than a misunderstanding, Tom. I'm getting more and more nervous about our school-master's fate.

TOM:

I think we should follow Master Crane's trail to the Van Tassel's. After all, it was their party he attended last night. We know he came to borrow a horse for the party. And we know he left to go to the party. Let's find out what he did while he was there.

   PIPER *begins to edge away.*

TOM:

Isn't it just over yonder?

   Notices PIPER *has slipped some distance away.*

Piper was just going to lead us, right?

PIPER:

Me? Why, this other path looks nice, too. Let's see where it leads.

TOM:

Piper, that path leads home.

PIPER:

I figured you'd point that out.

TOM:

If you go, you go alone. We're going to the Van Tassel's.

PIPER:

Sighs, resigned.

All right. It's this way.

PIPER *leads* TOM, MARY, *and* CROWD *to the next fire.*

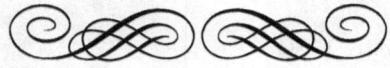

ACT THREE

TOM, MARY, *and* PIPER *enter the circle of the third fire, leading* CROWD.

MARY:

There it is. The Van Tassel house.

PIPER:

My pa says it's the grandest house in the county.

TOM:

I've never been inside. Have either of you?

MARY *and* PIPER *together:*

Never.

TOM:

Someone's coming this way.

Enter BALT *and* KATRINA *in distance.*

PIPER:

That's Mister Van Tassel.

MARY:

And his daughter Katrina. They must have been out for an evening walk.

TOM:

I think Master Crane came for more than just the Autumn Festival.

PIPER:

Like what?

TOM:

She's beautiful

MARY:

You think so? Do you think she's more beautiful than I am?

> MARY *primps.* TOM *ignores her, while* PIPER *considers.*

TOM:

I wondered why Master Crane had gone to all of the trouble of borrowing Van Ripper's horse and getting all dressed up.

PIPER:

Yes.

TOM:

Yes, what?

PIPER:

She is more beautiful than Mary.

MARY:

> *Hits* PIPER.

Ooh!

PIPER:

You asked! You shouldn't ask questions you don't want the answer to!

TOM:

C'mon, you two.

> TOM, MARY, *and* PIPER *meet* BALT. KATRINA *loiters behind.*

TOM:

Good evening, Mister Van Tassel.

BALT:

Evening, young man. Getting awfully late to be out of doors, don't you think?

TOM:

Sir, we're trying to find our school-master. This morning he did not show up for school. We know from Mister Van Ripper that he came last night to the Autumn Festival, but there's been no sign of him or the horse he rode.

   KATRINA *approaches.*

KATRINA:

What is it, Father?

BALT:

Katrina, my dear, these children and their friends have come searching for your singing teacher.

KATRINA:

Oh, how brave of you! I simply cannot believe that Mister Crane has disappeared. I worried I had-

   Stops abruptly, changes the subject.

We had heard, of course. Early today. News travels so quickly, you know, but this is so unlike him! He is a very responsible man.

TOM:

We're trying to find out what has happened to him.

BALT:

He certainly came to the Autumn Festival last night. People from all around Sleepy Hollow, and from Tarrytown, were in attendance.

Your school-master Crane entered as I talked with Jeremiah Acker.

BALT *moves to* PAST. *Enter* CRANE.

BALT:

Tells PRESENT.

He came straight to me and whisked my hand into his.

CRANE:

Shakes BALT'S *hand emphatically, exaggeratedly.*

Mister Van Tassel, Sir, a pleasure. An honor and a pleasure. And where, if I may be so bold, is your lovely daughter, that I may pay my respects immediately!

KATRINA:

Although I was across the room, I could hear myself as the subject of their discourse. I approached them.

KATRINA *moves to* PAST, *curtsies.*

KATRINA:

Well met, Mister Crane.

CRANE:

Ah, my lady Van Tassel.

Deep, exaggerated bow, sweeping her hand into his and brushing it against his lips.

It's been some time since we had our last singing lesson. I have missed the sound of your voice; my world feels like a forest absent of songbirds.

KATRINA:

Tells PRESENT; CRANE *pauses mid-bow.*

I must say I was most caught off guard by his behavior. Quite unpredictable. What do you think?

MARY:

Moves to the PAST *and examines the frozen* CRANE.

It appears to me that he is trying very hard to impress you.

KATRINA:

I had hoped the man was simply eccentric.

MARY *returns to* PRESENT.

KATRINA:

Mister Crane, please make use of our table and our food. I pray you will enjoy yourself.

CRANE:

If enjoying myself is your prayer, than I will make certain your prayers are answered. To disappoint you would be the worst catastrophe I can imagine!

KATRINA:

Oh, there are worse things, I am sure!

MARY:

Oh, he's got it bad.

PIPER:

That's how he talks to a lady? Is that how you're supposed to talk to a lady? Is that how I'm supposed to talk to you?

MARY:

Perhaps if you were a gentleman, but we don't have to worry about that.

BALT:

Tells PRESENT.

Ichabod proceeded to fill his plate, and eat.

KATRINA:

Also tells PRESENT.

And fill his plate...

BALT:

And eat.

KATRINA:

And fill his plate...

BALT:

And eat.

PIPER:

How many times did he go back?

KATRINA *and* BALT *simultaneously:*

I lost count.

CRANE:

Your wife is to be commended on setting a fine table. Every-thing was most excellent. Superior. Nonpareil.

BALT:

Thank you! I am sure she will be glad to hear of your satisfaction. Please, mingle. Enjoy yourself! Would you like some more to eat?

> *Period music begins to play.*

CRANE:

> *Taps leg enthusiastically.*

Ah! A band! I do so love music!

> *Approaches* KATRINA.

My lady, may I have this dance?

KATRINA:

Of course.

> *The dance is like a square dance, in which the partners face each other, clap, lock elbows, and promenade. Initially the two*

are matched in their moves, when suddenly CRANE *"gets down" in a most unusual manner. The contrast between* CRANE'S *dervish and* KATRINA'S *proper dancing styles is very evident.* BALT *claps while looking on, then moves back to* PRESENT.

BALT:

It was quite an unusual dance. Some kind of mixture between a tornado, a convulsion, and a, a, a-

PIPER:

Crane?

BALT:

Yes, exactly.

KATRINA:

My dear Ichabod! You dance most energetically!

CRANE:

Indeed, lady, I feel the music to the depths of my soul! Never let it be said that Ichabod Crane would not dance!

PIPER:

> *To* CROWD.

It is true that no one has ever suggested Master Crane would not dance. But hearing of this spectacle one must ask: could he dance? Or more importantly, should he?

BALT:

I believe Katrina would be dancing there still if Brom Bones had not cut in at the moment to sweep her away while Mister Crane executed a particularly grand rotation.

> CRANE *spins, cartwheels?* KATRINA *returns to* PRESENT, *hand on chest, winded.*

KATRINA:

Whew!

TOM:

Who is Brom Bones?

KATRINA:

He's such a mischievous soul. But he is good, I know! With a good heart! He saw me languishing with Mister Crane and swept me aside. "There, Miss Van Tassel," he said with a wink. "I have delivered you back to your guests."

>   BALT *returns to* PAST. CRANE *notices that* KATRINA *has gone; his dance winds down.*

KATRINA:

I thought perhaps Mister Crane would seek me out me again—but Father caught him and brought him to a group of the older men who were discussing some of the more popular local stories.

BALT:

Come, Mister Crane. I understand you are very interested in the spiritual haunts all around Sleepy Hollow.

CRANE:

>   *Distractedly.*

Indeed. Haunts?

BALT:

Yes, it's the time of year when the old fellows rekindle the ancient tales of the spirits roaming yon forest.

CRANE:

Mmm. How very intriguing. I am, after all, quite versed in Cotton Mather's account of the witches of Salem.

BALT:

Oh, that vile story of devilry!

KATRINA:

So my father, Mister Crane, and the other men discussed the stories of the spirits of Sleepy Hollow.

> BALT *leaves* CRANE; *returns to* PRESENT. CRANE *remains posed and silent.*

BALT:

I only stayed a moment, dear. But I heard later that Brom Bones gave a rather startling account of his meeting with the Headless Horseman.

TOM:

Headless Horseman?

BALT:

I wish I would have still been present at the table to hear his tale! I am so interested in the subject. I gather he had once met the Horseman along the Old Church Road.

PIPER:

What happened?

BALT:

Lad, I don't honestly know. Best to hear the story straight from Brom if you be curious on that account. A tale is best left to the teller.

KATRINA:

Quite right. We have, after all, left the subject of our discussion quite on his own.

> *Motions at* CRANE.

BALT:

As I was saying, I left Mister Crane with the local gentry and did not notice him until the evening had passed away, and so had the guests.

BALT *moves to* PAST.

Mister Crane, you seem quite distracted.

CRANE:

Distracted? What? Hmm. No, No, I'm not disfuddled, um, constracted. I mean, befused. I'm fine, really. Is Katrina near?

BALT:

She is seeing Brom off. The guests have all bidden us good night. You alone remain.

CRANE:

Indeed. I do! Then I must speak with her now. Yes, now...

KATRINA *moves to* PAST.

KATRINA:

Mister Crane, good evening to you. I pray for you a safe trip home. The servants go at once to find your horse and prepare the saddle for your ride.

CRANE:

Looks determined: pulls at coattails and inhales, as if preparing to act.

My lady! A word, if I may?

Turns away from crowd, though hands, shoulders, and lips still indicate that he is talking. KATRINA turns with him, her face still visible to the crowd in profile as she listens and nods and um-hums most attentively. It is obvious that the two are engaged in a conversation.

BALT:

To PRESENT.

He seemed quite bothered by something, as though plagued by voices in his head. I could only remember the stories I'd heard of Salem and the witches there. I was on edge, I must admit.

KATRINA:

Turning away from CRANE.

Sir, please, it is indeed late. You must be off! Not just because of my own entreaties, but for your own safety. Midnight approaches.

CRANE *looks at pocket watch.*

CRANE:

But Miss Van Tassel. Will you not consider my offer?

KATRINA:

I cannot at this time consider it. No sir, though I am honored, I will not consider it, though I do wish you well.

Exit a disheartened and crushed CRANE. KATRINA *and* BALT *re-enter* PRESENT, *delivering lines en route.*

BALT:

Offer? What offer? You spoke none of this before now?

KATRINA:

Father, there was no point airing my conversation with Mister Crane! It is sufficient to say we discussed a matter and he was disappointed with my answer.

BALT:

I am grieved to learn of it now! You should have told me!

KATRINA:

I am a grown woman with mind and wits. Half are inherited from you, and half from the woman you dote upon. Trust my judgment as you trust your own or my mother's.

BALT:

Shaking head.

Your eloquence leaves me speechless, as usual.

To children and CROWD.

So, children, there you have our story of Ichabod Crane's time at the festival. He left at, oh, I should say-

KATRINA:

Ten before midnight. I did so try to get him gone before the witching hour. He rode off along the Old Church Road.

PIPER:

Isn't that the haunt of the Galloping Hessian?

BALT:

Ah, you have sidestepped into a lecture, young man.

PIPER:

I have?

BALT:

Indeed, I've read many accounts and spoke with many a country man to discover that the Headless Horseman was no Hessian.

MARY:

Not a Hessian? But he led a troupe of Hessian mercenaries?

BALT:

He rode with that Hessian troupe–led them, yes, like the fiercest wolf of the pack. But he was no Hessian. Some folks who actually saw him thought he looked like a shaman from the orient. Others claimed he was a tattooed witch doctor out of wildest Africa. Some men recognized in him the style of an Iroquois medicine man. While others were sure he was of an old family of Italian gypsies. But it doesn't really matter where he came from because the stories begin to agree that he rode a ferocious black horse with eyes like blazing suns. And along the sides of his saddle hung his collection of painted skulls. That's right! Skulls, the heads of men he'd killed in battle. Two long chains of skulls hung, one on each side, and any who remembered seeing this rider could not remember his face, but only the clacking sound of the skulls rattling against their chains as he rode past.

And his sword! He carried at his side a great saber curved in the cavalry style so he could draw while riding and wave the shiny steel above his head.

But children! I forget myself when I get to talking about the Horseman! Now is not the time for tales of spirits! Come, it's late even now.

To KATRINA.

We should return to the house, and let these children run home. If the school-master has indeed disappeared, we should be all the more cautious until we know what has happened.

Good night, children.

MARY:

Thank you for telling us your story!

TOM *and* PIPER *simultaneously:*

Yes, thank you!

KATRINA:

Farewell!

MARY:

Well, how do you like that?

PIPER:

Like what?

MARY:

I know now what spirit had possession of Master Crane yesterday! Master Crane had his sights on Miss Van Tassel!

PIPER:

How do you know?

MARY:

Otherwise she would have told us what Master Crane said, of course. Since she didn't tell us, we know.

> PIPER *ponders this, seems to be on the verge of comprehension but not quite there.*

TOM:

She's a true lady, that one.

MARY:

She's a coquette. Did you see the way her eyes lit up when she talked of Brom Bones? Anyway, she's too old for you.

PIPER:

I don't know. Women live longer than men.

> MARY *hits* PIPER.

PIPER:

Ow. What's a coquette, anyway?

TOM:

C'mon.

PIPER:

Oh, good. I wondered when we'd head home. We should listen to Mister Van Tassel and-

TOM:

We're not going home yet.

PIPER:

We're not?

TOM:

First we're going to find Brom Bones.

MARY:

Brom Bones? Why?

TOM:

We need to learn what he told Master Crane last night.

PIPER:

Yea, but it was late an hour ago. Really, Tom, it's time for bed. Mary needs her beauty sleep.

    MARY *hits* PIPER *again.*

PIPER:

Okay, you don't! You don't!

    TOM, MARY, *and* PIPER *lead* CROWD *to the next fire.*

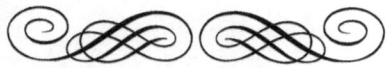

ACT FOUR

TOM, MARY, *and* PIPER *stop before entering the circle of the third fire.*

TOM:

What do you know about Brom Bones?

MARY:

He was christened Abraham Van Brunt and has lived in Sleepy Hollow all his days.

TOM:

So why is he called "Bones?"

MARY:

I've heard said he's an amazing horseman, but I can't figure how that has anything to do with "Bones." His horse Daredevil is notorious for its wickedness. He alone can handle the horse.

PIPER:

My dad said I should steer clear of Brom Bones and his gang. Said they were good for nothing but trouble.

TOM:

All right. We'll leave you here. In the woods. Alone. We'll be back to pick you up in, oh, say, half an hour.

PIPER:

Alarmed.

That's not funny, Tom!

MARY:

Up ahead! It's the Mott tavern.

BROM *waits at the fire as the group enters the circle.*

TOM:

And that group of folks outside?

PIPER:

Oh great. Sure enough, it's Abraham Van Brunt himself!

TOM:

Mister Van Brunt, sir!

BROM:

Eh? Mister Van Brunt? You're speaking to me, boy? Mister Van Brunt is my father. Call me Brom, lad! Just plain old Brom. And what are you all a thinkin' being out at this hour when all good folks are home?

PIPER:

> *Aside.*

That's what I keep wondering. Is my education really worth this?

TOM:

Sir, I mean, Brom, we're trying to figure out what happened to our school-master, Ichabod Crane. He never arrived for school this morning. We had heard that you may have talked to him last night, and we hoped you could help us discover his whereabouts.

BROM:

Oh, I heard word that the school-master had gone missing! A shame! A shame! It would be the Horseman, no doubt. I told him last night, and I thought he had enough wits to beware the wicked spirit who haunts Sleepy Hollow.

TOM:

So you think it was the Headless Horseman? But isn't that just an old tale? Something told to frighten children around the flickering light of a campfire?

BROM:

Laughs.

Just a story, lad? No, the Horseman is far more than any old story. What do you know of the Horseman?

TOM:

Well, what everybody knows, I guess. The Headless Horseman is a ghost that rides the Old Church Road searching for his lost head.

PIPER:

And Mister Van Tassel said he wasn't really a Hessian, but something else; something no one could figure out as anything. Isn't that so?

BROM:

That's all you heard? No wonder you don't know any better and come out at night when God fearin' folk stay indoors.

TOM:

You're outside!

BROM:

I'm Brom Bones! My family has a long history with that goblin, from my Great Grandfather on down to myself. But you might wish you were a home by the time I'm finished telling you my story. You see, I've met the Horseman, indeed I have, and if you'll come closer, I'll tell you about it, as I did your school-master Crane last night. Come closer, c'mon. You might as well get comfortable, because this story isn't.

> TOM, MARY, PIPER, *and* CROWD *gather round* BROM;
> the three players *seat themselves on logs.* CRANE *enters*
> PAST *during* BROM'S *introduction.*

Yes, indeed, last night we talked at length about the local
spirits and haunts. Your school-master was there, and old
Baltus Van Tassel, and many others of the local gentry, their
wives, sons, and daughters. Crane had just finished explaining something that I don't rightly pretend to remember. It had
to do with-

> BROM *and* CRANE *begin their lines simultaneously, with*
> CRANE'S *line flowing into a school-master's lecture.*

BROM:

Cotton Mather.

CRANE:

Cotton Mather's great book is our evidence. Our worldly
bodies are beset upon all sides by evil spirits seeking to collect
us for their master!

> *Waves a finger in emphasis.*

BROM:

> *Frowning, remembering.*

I think. Or maybe it was-

BROM *and* CRANE *again begin simultaneously:*

-bodies of water.

CRANE:

-are like poison to spirits; they can't cross them, or touch
them, and holy water is the purest of poisons to them!

BROM:

No! I remember, now. He was explaining about-

BROM *and* CRANE *simultaneously:*

Psalms-

CRANE:

-can strengthen a quivering heart. As I walk the long wooded paths of Sleepy Hollow and am beset by the spirits of evil, I sing loud the Psalms of our Lord. Ghostly fingers can find no handhold upon the glassy word of God! 'Tis a great fortification of spirit.

BROM:

Moves into PAST to ask incredulously.

So you have met spirits as you meander to and fro?

CRANE:

Of course! I am certain we all have. You yourself must have, most certainly.

BROM:

Incredulity becomes smugness as Brom appears to have an idea.

I? Yes, I did once meet the Horseman.

CRANE:

The Headless Horseman of Sleepy Hollow? The Galloping Hessian? Indeed, say more, say more!

As BROM relates the story, CRANE'S body language, both his face and stance, becomes increasingly terrified.

BROM:

It's not a story I like to repeat. Reliving those moments is uncomfortable; but as you have entreated me, I shall share my version of events.

It was a night not unlike this one: an autumn night, and the moon hung full in the sky, breathing her milky breath upon the countryside. I was on my way back from Sing Sing, and had run later than I expected. I rode Daredevil at a steady pace and his hooves clicked and clacked like a resting heart-beat. But in an instant I felt my own heart palpitations increase two-fold; from behind came the matched clatter of another horse's hooves. Who could this new rider be, at midnight, when all the world is sound asleep and only fools on fools' errands are out? I turned to look behind, and saw only a shape of shadow, a great bundled mass of darkness astride a beast most ferocious in countenance. Closer came the shadowy figure on horseback. I urged Daredevil to a trot. Behind me the horseman did the same, matching my own steed's pace hoof for hoof.

My suspicions about this rider were kindled, and a great fear settled. Could this be the Horseman of Sleepy Hollow, of whom so many tales are told, I wondered. Could this rider be seeking my head, to replace that which he had lost those many years ago? And what if it was not the Horseman, but some local yokel out to prank or joke? A plot entered my brain, a method whereby I could determine if I was followed by man or goblin. "I will race you to the Church-bridge!" I declared to the rider. "For a bowl of punch, I will race you and we shall see who the faster horseman is!"

Without waiting for answer, I leapt to the race, pushing Daredevil to his limits. Behind me the Horseman galloped as well. While aware of his steed's nostrils at my back, I tried ever harder to guide Daredevil over the uneven ground. Daredevil put on a great show of speed, being a fiercer horse than most. We neared the Church-bridge, and the Horseman had not yet overtaken me. A feeling of pride surged within me and I turned to take in the shape of my pursuer.

There, behind me, silhouetted in the moonlight, rode the body of a man, and where the head should be, there was nothing: a shelf of shoulders empty of neck, jaw and skull. No eyes to see me, no mouth to answer me, no ears to hear me, but a powerful body, and a powerful steed. In that instant Daredevil floundered as the Horseman burst in speed. He passed me up! In his hand, I saw as he held it aloft, a head–a disembodied head. I could make out none of the features, you understand, but its shape was unmistakable. Holding that head like a token of power he threw it at me. I reigned Daredevil hard up and the Horseman erupted in a flash of light, disappearing as his horse stepped foot upon the wood of the Church-bridge.

You were correct, Mister Crane, that the spirit could not pass the water. When he raced onto the bridge he banished himself for the night.

I looked for that head, that orphaned member, but found nothing. To this day I fear knowing whose head it was that he threw at me.

CRANE:

Working his jaw as though in search of his voice until finally:

A fearsome tale.

Clears throat.

A prescription of Psalms will boost you up. I shall share one with you even now-

BROM:

Nay, nay. I am quite recovered. It was some time ago, and my wits have been quite salved by the lush table of our good host, Baltus Van Tassel. Here's a cheer to our host!

Lifts invisible glass.

May his table never lack, may his fields never lack, and may his family never lack!

CRANE *lifts his own imaginary glass in the toast.*

BROM *and* CRANE:

Here, Here!

BROM:

> *To* PRESENT.

He seemed quite shaken by my tale.

PIPER:

Who wouldn't be?

BROM:

It was much later when I left, and saw that your school-master was still sampling food from the table.

BROM:

Crane, remember my tale! Don't find yourself out too late along the Old Church Road! The Horseman, my man! It is best to avoid him at all costs! You will be hard pressed to sing psalms while racing neck to neck with him.

> *Grabs throat dramatically and pretends to have difficulty swallowing.*

CRANE:

Of course. Of course. But first I must find Katrina.

BROM:

Those were the last words I spoke to him: a warning. And he did not show up at the schoolhouse for lessons?

TOM:

No, indeed. And it's as though no one in Sleepy Hollow is surprised or concerned. It's like another day in which nothing unusual has taken place.

BROM:

In Sleepy Hollow, the unusual is usual, my boy. This land's been rife with spirits since long before the white man came here. The Indian legends of witchmen and wizards have taught that night in this valley is a time for spirits, not flesh and bone, to be afoot. That's why you're not convincing all of the local folks to scour the woods. They know what rides the roads when the moon rises, and they know too that no Psalm is armor for the neck. A good fire, a warm bed, a prayer to the Lord above, these are the habits of Sleepy Hollow folk. Go home children, and leave these inquiries for the daytime.

TOM, MARY, *and* PIPER:

We will!

Exit Brom.

TOM:

But first-

PIPER:

No! Are you mad?

TOM:

First we should just follow the road up to the Church-bridge. Katrina said he left her house and went to along the Old Church Road.

PIPER:

Were we listening to the same story?

MARY:

Tom, Piper is right for once. We should get home.

TOM:

We're more than halfway there. Besides, it's not too late. We should still be safe.

PIPER:

Should!

MARY:

I'll agree to this, but if I see the Horseman I will run, ducking the whole time. In fact, we should all duck, or experience the most tragic of partings.

TOM:

I'll hold my head high. I won't let anything happen to you.

TOM, MARY, *and* PIPER *lead* CROWD *to the final act.*

ACT FIVE

TOM, MARY, *and* PIPER *lead* CROWD *toward the bridge.*

TOM:

It seems peaceful here.

PIPER:

I feel like I'm standing in the Old Dutch Cemetery.

MARY:

It's chilly. Not the same thing as cold, mind you, but chilly in a way I feel down to my toes.

TOM:

Look, the Church-bridge. See, we're not far now!

PIPER:

What's that? Do you hear something?

TOM:

No, Piper, it's just your imagination.

MARY:

I don't know.

TOM:

Mary, not you, too!

PIPER:

Those are hoof beats.

TOM:

No, they're not. Well, even if they are, that doesn't mean they belong to a ghost. Some-body could be riding along the road. Really, I'm sure some body is riding along the road, not a headless spirit. What's the likelihood-

PIPER:

At night, in Sleepy Hollow, I'd say there's a good likelihood.

MARY:

It's the Horseman!

> *Behind* TOM, MARY, PIPER *and* CROWD, THE HORSEMAN *sits astride his steed, a silhouette in the distance. He dramatically pulls a cavalry sword from its sheath at his belt and holds it threateningly high, then points it at* CROWD, TOM, MARY, *and* PIPER. PIPER *collapses.*

MARY:

> *Stooping to help Piper to his feet.*

I said we should "duck," not faint.

> TOM *hurriedly helps* MARY *with* PIPER. PIPER *stands, looks towards* THE HORSEMAN *again.*

PIPER:

Aaah!

> PIPER *races toward the bridge full-speed. Pie pumpkins line both edges of the bridge.*

TOM:

Across the Church-bridge! Follow Piper! Everybody, across the Church-bridge! The spirit can't cross the water!

> THE HORSEMAN *advances on* CROWD *waving the sword.* CROWD *moves toward bridge.* PIPER *leads;* TOM *and* MARY *take the rear.*

PIPER:

Let's go, everybody! Hurry up! If we can get to the bridge, we'll be safe!

MARY:

Duck! Don't lose your heads! Duck!

THE HORSEMAN *nears* CROWD; *some are on the bridge.*

MARY:

Behind CROWD, MARY *falls.*

Oh-

TOM:

Mary! Oh, no!

TOM *races to* MARY *while continuing to prompt* CROWD.

Duck! Get Across the Church-bridge and keep your heads down!

TOM *races to* MARY *and stoops to help her.* THE HORSE-MAN *should nearly catch the last of* CROWD, *then turn to* TOM *and* MARY. THE HORSEMAN *stands between* TOM, *who is leaning over the fallen* MARY, *and the safety of the bridge.* TOM *pulls* MARY *to her feet.* THE HORSE-MAN *points his sword at them.* CROWD *has, by this time, crossed the bridge and watches from the far side.*

PIPER:

Oh, no! I've got to do something.

PIPER *stoops to pick up a pumpkin and then carries it back off the bridge toward* THE HORSEMAN.

Hey, look here! I've found your head! Little worse for the wear but just fine!

THE HORSEMAN *is distracted by* PIPER. TOM *and* MARY *take advantage of his distraction to move behind his back toward the bridge.*

PIPER:

Here you go!

Throws the pumpkin away from TOM *and* MARY *and the bridge into some brush, where its fall will be hidden from* CROWD.

The answer to your nightly search!

THE HORSEMAN *moves off after the pumpkin, giving* TOM *and* MARY *just enough time to slip over the bridge to safety.* PIPER *helps them across and as he does so,* THE HORSE-MAN *returns to the entrance to the bridge. He has sheathed his sword and carries a pumpkin–it's meant to be the same pumpkin* PIPER *threw, but if* PIPER'S *actually broke,* THE HORSEMAN *will need to have a new pumpkin to carry.* THE HORSEMAN *holds the pumpkin aloft, and silently, angrily, throws it across the bridge at* TOM, MARY, PIPER, *and* CROWD. *Then* THE HORSEMAN *rears, turns about, and races away. Yes, this will mean cleaning pumpkin guts from the bridge between shows.*

PIPER:

What do you think about our fairy stories now?

TOM:

I don't know what to think. I was so sure-

MARY:

You saw him with your own eyes!

TOM:

Master Crane, for all his book learning, alone along that road last night- What chance did he really stand against such a spirit?

MARY:

He almost got us. Piper's quick thinking was the only thing that saved us.

PIPER:

Quick thinking? Me? So that's what quick thinking is like. I've often wondered.

MARY:

The road continues through the hallowed grounds of the Old Dutch Church. We should be able to follow this road around Sleepy Hollow and return home that way.

PIPER:

So it's finally time to go home?

TOM:

   To CROWD.

When we gathered earlier, I was sorely disappointed to see so few to search for Master Crane. But you stayed with us, even after hearing Van Ripper warn us from our search. After Brom Bones's tale of the Headless Horseman, you remained, even up to the Church-bridge.

Tonight we have escaped the Headless Horseman of Sleepy Hollow! I couldn't have asked for more bravery from any folks. Now, though, I must admit that Mary and Piper were right: we should not be out in these woods after dark. I've learned my lesson, and it's one I'll keep with me for the rest of my days. I pray that you all will heed the warning to beware the witching hour!

MARY:

Thank you all for coming, and please be careful as you follow the roads home. Don't cross the water to the other side of the creek before daylight. And most importantly: remember to duck!

PIPER:

Wouldn't it be funny if people started seeing the Horseman riding around with a pumpkin on his head. I mean, can you imagine that?

MARY:

Piper, that's the most ridiculous idea you've had all night.

PIPER:

But it's funny, right? Right?

TOM, MARY, *and* PIPER:

Good night, everybody.

> *Exit all.*

THE LEGEND OF SLEEPY HOLLOW
Washington Irving

A Note on the Preparation of This Edition

The Legend of Sleepy Hollow was specially prepared for this publication from an original scan of a public domain book from my own library: *The Sketch Book* by Washington Irving, edited by George Philip Krapp, published by Scott Foresman and Company in 1920 as a part of *The Lake English Classics*. Three alternate public domain editions were consulted for consistency.

No attempt was made to modernize Irving's spelling or punctuation. As with any digitization process, errors or inaccuracies can occur and are unintentional.

The footnotes are my own (except for Irving's footnote about the Whip-poor-will, which uses * instead of numbers) and did not appear in the Krapp edition. They were included to help the reader enjoy the story without resorting to a dictionary, encyclopedia, or (as is more likely) the Internet.

A.W.

THE LEGEND OF SLEEPY HOLLOW.
FOUND AMONG THE PAPERS OF THE LATE DIEDRICH KNICKERBOCKER.

> A pleasing land of drowsy head it was,
>> Of dreams that wave before the half-shut eye;
>> And of gay castles in the clouds that pass,
>> For ever flushing round a summer sky.
>>> CASTLE OF INDOLENCE.[1]

In the bosom of one of those spacious coves which indent the eastern shore of the Hudson, at that broad expansion of the river denominated[2] by the ancient Dutch navigators the Tappan Zee, and where they always prudently shortened sail, and implored the protection of St. Nicholas when they crossed, there lies a small market-town or rural port, which by some is called Greensburgh, but which is more generally and properly known by the name of Tarry Town. This name was given, we are told, in former days, by the good housewives of the adjacent country, from the inveterate propensity of their husbands to linger about the village tavern on market days. Be that as it may, I do not vouch for the fact, but merely advert to it, for the sake of being precise and authentic. Not far from this village, perhaps about two miles, there is a little valley, or rather lap of land, among high hills, which is one of the quietest places in the whole world. A small brook glides through it, with just murmur enough to lull one to repose; and the occasional whistle of a quail, or tapping of a wood-pecker, is almost the only sound that ever breaks in upon the uniform tranquillity.

I recollect that, when a stripling, my first exploit in squirrel-shooting was in a grove of tall walnut-trees that shades one side of the valley. I had wandered into it at noon time, when

---

[1] A poem published in 1748 by James Thomson.
[2] Named.

all nature is peculiarly quiet, and was startled by the roar of my own gun, as it broke the Sabbath stillness around, and was prolonged and reverberated by the angry echoes. If ever I should wish for a retreat, whither I might steal from the world and its distractions, and dream quietly away the remnant of a troubled life, I know of none more promising than this little valley.

From the listless repose of the place, and the peculiar character of its inhabitants, who are descendants from the original Dutch settlers, this sequestered glen has long been known by the name of SLEEPY HOLLOW, and its rustic lads are called the Sleepy Hollow Boys throughout all the neighboring country. A drowsy, dreamy influence seems to hang over the land, and to pervade the very atmosphere. Some say that the place was bewitched by a high German doctor, during the early days of the settlement; others, that an old Indian chief, the prophet or wizard of his tribe, held his pow-wows there before the country was discovered by Master Hendrick Hudson. Certain it is, the place still continues under the sway of some witching power, that holds a spell over the minds of the good people, causing them to walk in a continual reverie. They are given to all kinds of marvellous beliefs; are subject to trances and visions; and frequently see strange sights, and hear music and voices in the air. The whole neighborhood abounds with vocal tales, haunted spots, and twilight superstitions; stars shoot and meteors glare oftener across the valley than in any other part of the country, and the nightmare, with her whole ninefold, seems to make it the favorite scene of her gambols. The dominant spirit, however, that haunts this enchanted region, and seems to be commander-in-chief of all the powers of the air, is the apparition of a figure on horseback without head. It is said by some to be the ghost of a Hessian[3] trooper, whose head had been carried away by a cannon-ball, in some

---

[3] Many of the German mercenaries hired by the British during the Revolutionary War were from the province of Hesse-Cassel and were called "Hessians."

nameless battle during the revolutionary war; and who is ever
and anon seen by the country folk, hurrying along in the
gloom of night, as if on the wings of the wind. His haunts are
not confined to the valley, but extend at times to the adjacent
roads, and especially to the vicinity of a church at no great
distance. Indeed, certain of the most authentic historians of
those parts, who have been careful in collecting and collating
the floating facts concerning this spectre, allege that the body
of the trooper, having been buried in the church-yard, the
ghost rides forth to the scene of battle in nightly quest of his
head; and that the rushing speed with which he sometimes
passes along the Hollow, like a midnight blast, is owing to his
being belated, and in a hurry to get back to the church-yard
before daybreak.

Such is the general purport of this legendary superstition,
which has furnished materials for many a wild story in that
region of shadows; and the spectre is known, at all the country
firesides, by the name of the Headless Horseman of Sleepy
Hollow.

It is remarkable that the visionary propensity I have mentioned is not confined to the native inhabitants of the valley,
but is unconsciously imbibed by every one who resides there
for a time. However wide awake they may have been before
they entered that sleepy region, they are sure, in a little time,
to inhale the witching influence of the air, and begin to grow
imaginative—to dream dreams, and see apparitions.

I mention this peaceful spot with all possible laud; for it is
in such little retired Dutch valleys, found here and there
embosomed in the great State of New York, that population,
manners, and customs, remain fixed; while the great torrent
of migration and improvement, which is making such inces-
sant changes in other parts of this restless country, sweeps by
them unobserved. They are like those little nooks of still
water which border a rapid stream; where we may see the
straw and bubble riding quietly at anchor, or slowly revolving
in their mimic harbor, undisturbed by the rush of the passing

current. Though many years have elapsed since I trod the drowsy shades of Sleepy Hollow, yet I question whether I should not still find the same trees and the same families vegetating in its sheltered bosom.

In this by-place of nature, there abode, in a remote period of American history, that is to say, some thirty years since, a worthy wight[4] of the name of Ichabod Crane; who sojourned, or, as he expressed it, "tarried," in Sleepy Hollow, for the purpose of instructing the children of the vicinity. He was a native of Connecticut; a State which supplies the Union with pioneers for the mind as well as for the forest, and sends forth yearly its legions of frontier woodsmen and country school-masters. The cognomen[5] of Crane was not inapplicable to his person. He was tall, but exceedingly lank, with narrow shoulders, long arms and legs, hands that dangled a mile out of his sleeves, feet that might have served for shovels, and his whole frame most loosely hung together. His head was small, and flat at top, with huge ears, large green glassy eyes, and a long snipe nose, so that it looked like a weather-cock, perched upon his spindle neck, to tell which way the wind blew. To see him striding along the profile of a hill on a windy day, with his clothes bagging and fluttering about him, one might have mistaken him for the genius of famine descending upon the earth, or some scarecrow eloped from a cornfield.

His school-house was a low building of one large room, rudely constructed of logs; the windows partly glazed, and partly patched with leaves of old copy-books. It was most ingeniously secured at vacant hours, by a withe[6] twisted in the handle of the door, and stakes set against the window shutters; so that, though a thief might get in with perfect ease, he would find some embarrassment in getting out; an idea most probably borrowed by the architect, Yost Van Houten, from

---

[4] Person or creature.
[5] Surname.
[6] A willow branch used for tying.

the mystery of an eel-pot.[7] The school-house stood in a rather lonely but pleasant situation, just at the foot of a woody hill, with a brook running close by, and a formidable birch tree growing at one end of it. From hence the low murmur of his pupils' voices, conning[8] over their lessons, might be heard in a drowsy summer's day, like the hum of a bee-hive; interrupted now and then by the authoritative voice of the master, in the tone of menace or command; or, peradventure, by the appalling sound of the birch, as he urged some tardy loiterer along the flowery path of knowledge. Truth to say, he was a conscientious man, and ever bore in mind the golden maxim, "Spare the rod and spoil the child."—Ichabod Crane's scholars certainly were not spoiled.

I would not have it imagined, however, that he was one of those cruel potentates[9] of the school, who joy in the smart[10] of their subjects; on the contrary, he administered justice with discrimination rather than severity; taking the burthen[11] off the backs of the weak, and laying it on those of the strong. Your mere puny stripling, that winced at the least flourish of the rod, was passed by with indulgence; but the claims of justice were satisfied by inflicting a double portion on some little, tough, wrong-headed, broad-skirted Dutch urchin, who sulked and swelled and grew dogged and sullen beneath the birch. All this he called "doing his duty by their parents;" and he never inflicted a chastisement without following it by the assurance, so consolatory to the smarting urchin, that "he would remember it, and thank him for it the longest day he had to live."

When school hours were over, he was even the companion and playmate of the larger boys; and on holiday afternoons would convoy some of the smaller ones home, who happened

---

[7] A basket-like trap that lets eels in but keeps them from getting out.
[8] Study or learn by heart.
[9] Ruler.
[10] In this context, pain, e.g. "Ow! That smarted."
[11] Archaic version of "burden."

to have pretty sisters, or good housewives for mothers, noted for the comforts of the cupboard. Indeed it behooved him to keep on good terms with his pupils. The revenue arising from his school was small, and would have been scarcely sufficient to furnish him with daily bread, for he was a huge feeder, and though lank, had the dilating powers of an anaconda; but to help out his maintenance, he was, according to country custom in those parts, boarded and lodged at the houses of the farmers, whose children he instructed. With these he lived successively a week at a time; thus going the rounds of the neighborhood, with all his worldly effects tied up in a cotton handkerchief.

That all this might not be too onerous on the purses of his rustic patrons, who are apt to consider the costs of schooling a grievous burden,[12] and schoolmasters as mere drones, he had various ways of rendering himself both useful and agreeable. He assisted the farmers occasionally in the lighter labors of their farms; helped to make hay; mended the fences; took the horses to water; drove the cows from pasture; and cut wood for the winter fire. He laid aside, too, all the dominant dignity and absolute sway with which he lorded it in his little empire, the school, and became wonderfully gentle and ingratiating. He found favor in the eyes of the mothers, by petting the children, particularly the youngest; and like the lion bold, which whilom[13] so magnanimously the lamb did hold, he would sit with a child on one knee, and rock a cradle with his foot for whole hours together.

In addition to his other vocations, he was the singing-master of the neighborhood, and picked up many bright shillings by instructing the young folks in psalmody.[14] It was a matter of no little vanity to him, on Sundays, to take his station in front of the church gallery, with a band of chosen

---

[12] Irving uses both "burthen" and "burden" in this story, though some editions replace the archaic "burthen" with the modern "burden."
[13] Formerly.
[14] Singing of Psalms.

singers; where, in his own mind, he completely carried away the palm from the parson. Certain it is, his voice resounded far above all the rest of the congregation; and there are peculiar quavers still to be heard in that church, and which may even be heard half a mile off, quite to the opposite side of the mill-pond, on a still Sunday morning, which are said to be legitimately descended from the nose of Ichabod Crane. Thus, by divers little make-shifts in that ingenious way which is commonly denominated "by hook and by crook," the worthy pedagogue[15] got on tolerably enough, and was thought, by all who understood nothing of the labor of headwork, to have a wonderfully easy life of it.

The schoolmaster is generally a man of some importance in the female circle of a rural neighborhood; being considered a kind of idle gentlemanlike personage, of vastly superior taste and accomplishments to the rough country swains, and, indeed, inferior in learning only to the parson. His appearance, therefore, is apt to occasion some little stir at the tea-table of a farmhouse, and the addition of a supernumerary[16] dish of cakes or sweetmeats, or, peradventure, the parade of a silver tea-pot. Our man of letters, therefore, was peculiarly happy in the smiles of all the country damsels. How he would figure among them in the church-yard, between services on Sundays! gathering grapes for them from the wild vines that overrun the surrounding trees; reciting for their amusement all the epitaphs on the tombstones; or sauntering, with a whole bevy of them, along the banks of the adjacent mill-pond; while the more bashful country bumpkins hung sheepishly back, envying his superior elegance and address.

From his half itinerant life, also, he was a kind of travelling gazette, carrying the whole budget of local gossip from house to house; so that his appearance was always greeted with satisfaction. He was, moreover, esteemed by the women as a

---

[15] A pedantic teacher, especially one who is overly concerned with minor details.
[16] Extra.

man of great erudition,[17] for he had read several books quite through, and was a perfect master of Cotton Mather's history of New England Witchcraft, in which, by the way, he most firmly and potently believed.

He was, in fact, an odd mixture of small shrewdness and simple credulity. His appetite for the marvellous, and his powers of digesting it, were equally extraordinary; and both had been increased by his residence in this spellbound region. No tale was too gross or monstrous for his capacious swallow. It was often his delight, after his school was dismissed in the afternoon, to stretch himself on the rich bed of clover, bordering the little brook that whimpered by his school-house, and there con over old Mather's direful tales, until the gathering dusk of the evening made the printed page a mere mist before his eyes. Then, as he wended his way, by swamp and stream and awful woodland, to the farmhouse where he happened to be quartered, every sound of nature, at that witching hour, fluttered his excited imagination: the moan of the whip-poor-will* from the hill-side; the boding cry of the tree-toad, that harbinger of storm; the dreary hooting of the screech-owl, or the sudden rustling in the thicket of birds frightened from their roost. The fire-flies, too, which sparkled most vividly in the darkest places, now and then startled him, as one of uncommon brightness would stream across his path; and if, by chance, a huge blockhead of a beetle came winging his blundering flight against him, the poor varlet[18] was ready to give up the ghost, with the idea that he was struck with a witch's token. His only resource on such occasions, either to drown thought, or drive away evil spirits, was to sing psalm tunes;— and the good people of Sleepy Hollow, as they sat by their doors of an evening, were often filled with awe, at hearing his

---

[17] Knowledge or learning.

* The whip-poor-will is a bird which is only heard at night. It receives its name from its note, which is thought to resemble those words.

[18] A servant.

nasal melody, "in linked sweetness long drawn out," floating from the distant hill, or along the dusky road.

Another of his sources of fearful pleasure was, to pass long winter evenings with the old Dutch wives, as they sat spinning by the fire, with a row of apples roasting and spluttering along the hearth, and listen to their marvellous tales of ghosts and goblins, and haunted fields, and haunted brooks, and haunted bridges, and haunted houses, and particularly of the headless horseman, or galloping Hessian of the Hollow, as they sometimes called him. He would delight them equally by his anecdotes of witchcraft, and of the direful omens and portentous sights and sounds in the air, which prevailed in the earlier times of Connecticut; and would frighten them wofully with speculations upon comets and shooting stars; and with the alarming fact that the world did absolutely turn round, and that they were half the time topsy-turvy!

But if there was a pleasure in all this, while snugly cuddling in the chimney corner of a chamber that was all of a ruddy glow from the crackling wood fire, and where, of course, no spectre dared to show his face, it was dearly purchased by the terrors of his subsequent walk homewards. What fearful shapes and shadows beset his path amidst the dim and ghastly glare of a snowy night!—With what wistful look did he eye every trembling ray of light streaming across the waste fields from some distant window!—How often was he appalled by some shrub covered with snow, which, like a sheeted spectre, beset his very path!—How often did he shrink with curdling awe at the sound of his own steps on the frosty crust beneath his feet; and dread to look over his shoulder, lest he should behold some uncouth being tramping close behind him!—and how often was he thrown into complete dismay by some rushing blast, howling among the trees, in the idea that it was the Galloping Hessian on one of his nightly scourings!

All these, however, were mere terrors of the night, phantoms of the mind that walk in darkness; and though he had seen many spectres in his time, and been more than once

beset by Satan in divers shapes, in his lonely perambula-
tions,[19] yet daylight put an end to all these evils; and he would
have passed a pleasant life of it, in despite of the devil and all
his works, if his path had not been crossed by a being that
causes more perplexity to mortal man than ghosts, goblins,
and the whole race of witches put together, and that was—a
woman.

Among the musical disciples who assembled, one evening
in each week, to receive his instructions in psalmody, was
Katrina Van Tassel, the daughter and only child of a substantial Dutch farmer. She was a blooming lass of fresh eighteen;
plump as a partridge; ripe and melting and rosy cheeked as
one of her father's peaches; and universally famed, not merely
for her beauty, but her vast expectations. She was withal a
little of a coquette,[20] as might be perceived even in her dress,
which was a mixture of ancient and modern fashions, as most
suited to set off her charms. She wore the ornaments of pure
yellow gold, which her great-great-grandmother had brought
over from Saardam;[21] the tempting stomacher[22] of the olden
time; and withal a provokingly short petticoat, to display the
prettiest foot and ankle in the country round.[23]

Ichabod Crane had a soft and foolish heart towards the sex;
and it is not to be wondered at, that so tempting a morsel soon
found favor in his eyes; more especially after he had visited
her in her paternal mansion. Old Baltus Van Tassel was a
perfect picture of a thriving, contented, liberal-hearted
farmer. He seldom, it is true, sent either his eyes or his
thoughts beyond the boundaries of his own farm; but within
those every thing was snug, happy, and well-conditioned. He
was satisfied with his wealth, but not proud of it; and piqued
himself upon the hearty abundance, rather than the style in

---

[19] Wanderings.
[20] A flirt.
[21] A town in Holland.
[22] A V-shaped cloth that covers the chest and stomach, originally fashionable for men and women in the 16th century, but subsequently worn only by women.
[23] Contrast this with today's fashions!

which he lived. His stronghold was situated on the banks of the Hudson, in one of those green, sheltered, fertile nooks, in which the Dutch farmers are so fond of nestling. A great elm-tree spread its broad branches over it; at the foot of which bubbled up a spring of the softest and sweetest water, in a little well, formed of a barrel; and then stole sparkling away through the grass, to a neighboring brook, that bubbled along among alders and dwarf willows. Hard by the farmhouse was a vast barn, that might have served for a church; every window and crevice of which seemed bursting forth with the treasures of the farm; the flail was busily resounding within it from morning to night; swallows and martins skimmed twittering about the eaves; and rows of pigeons, some with one eye turned up, as if watching the weather, some with their heads under their wings or buried in their bosoms, and others swelling, and cooing, and bowing about their dames, were enjoying the sunshine on the roof. Sleek unwieldy porkers were grunting in the repose and abundance of their pens; whence sallied forth, now and then, troops of sucking pigs, as if to snuff the air. A stately squadron of snowy geese were riding in an adjoining pond, convoying whole fleets of ducks; regiments of turkeys were gobbling through the farmyard, and guinea fowls fretting about it, like ill-tempered housewives, with their peevish discontented cry. Before the barn door strutted the gallant cock, that pattern of a husband, a warrior, and a fine gentleman, clapping his burnished wings, and crowing in the pride and gladness of his heart—sometimes tearing up the earth with his feet, and then generously calling his ever-hungry family of wives and children to enjoy the rich morsel which he had discovered.

The pedagogue's mouth watered, as he looked upon this sumptuous promise of luxurious winter fare. In his devouring mind's eye, he pictured to himself every roasting-pig running about with a pudding in his belly, and an apple in his mouth; the pigeons were snugly put to bed in a comfortable pie, and tucked in with a coverlet of crust; the geese were swimming in their own gravy; and the ducks pairing cosily in dishes, like snug married couples, with a decent competency of onion sauce. In the porkers he saw carved out the future sleek side of bacon, and juicy relishing ham; not a turkey but he beheld daintily trussed up, with its gizzard under its wing, and, per-adventure, a necklace of savory sausages; and even bright chanticleer himself lay sprawling on his back, in a side-dish, with uplifted claws, as if craving that quarter which his chivalrous spirit disdained to ask while living.

As the enraptured Ichabod fancied all this, and as he rolled his great green eyes over the fat meadow-lands, the rich fields of wheat, of rye, of buckwheat, and Indian corn, and the orchards burthened with ruddy fruit which surrounded the warm tenement of Van Tassel, his heart yearned after the damsel who was to inherit these domains, and his imagination expanded with the idea, how they might be readily turned into cash, and the money invested in immense tracts of wild land, and shingle palaces in the wilderness. Nay, his busy fancy already realized his hopes, and presented to him the blooming Katrina, with a whole family of children, mounted on the top of a wagon loaded with household trumpery, with pots and kettles dangling beneath; and he beheld himself bestriding a pacing mare, with a colt at her heels, setting out for Kentucky, Tennessee, or the Lord knows where.

When he entered the house the conquest of his heart was complete. It was one of those spacious farmhouses, with high-ridged, but lowly-sloping roofs, built in the style handed down from the first Dutch settlers; the low projecting eaves forming a piazza along the front, capable of being closed up in bad weather. Under this were hung flails, harness, various utensils of husbandry, and nets for fishing in the neighboring river. Benches were built along the sides for summer use, and a great spinning-wheel at one end, and a churn at the other, showed the various uses to which this important porch might be devoted. From this piazza the wondering Ichabod entered the hall, which formed the centre of the mansion and the place of usual residence. Here, rows of resplendent pewter, ranged on a long dresser, dazzled his eyes. In one corner stood a huge bag of wool ready to be spun; in another a quantity of linsey-woolsey just from the loom; ears of Indian corn, and strings of dried apples and peaches, hung in gay festoons along the walls, mingled with the gaud of red peppers; and a door left ajar gave him a peep into the best parlor, where the claw-footed chairs, and dark mahogany tables, shone like mirrors; and irons, with their accompanying shovel and tongs, glistened from their covert of asparagus tops; mock-oranges and conch-shells decorated the mantelpiece; strings of various colored birds' eggs were suspended above it: a great ostrich egg was hung from the centre of the room, and a corner cupboard, knowingly left open, displayed immense treasures of old silver and well-mended china.

From the moment Ichabod laid his eyes upon these regions of delight, the peace of his mind was at an end, and his only study was how to gain the affections of the peerless daughter of Van Tassel. In this enterprise, however, he had more real difficulties than generally fell to the lot of a knight-errant of yore, who seldom had any thing but giants, enchanters, fiery dragons, and such like easily-conquered adversaries, to contend with; and had to make his way merely through gates of iron and brass, and walls of adamant, to the castle keep, where the lady of his heart was confined, all which he achieved as easily as a man would carve his way to the centre of a Christmas pie; and then the lady gave him her hand as a matter of course. Ichabod, on the contrary, had to win his way to the heart of a country coquette, beset with a labyrinth of whims and caprices, which were for ever presenting new difficulties and impediments; and he had to encounter a host of fearful adversaries of real flesh and blood, the numerous rustic admirers, who beset every portal to her heart; keeping a watchful and angry eye upon each other, but ready to fly out in the common cause against any new competitor.

Among these the most formidable was a burly, roaring, roystering blade, of the name of Abraham, or, according to the Dutch abbreviation, Brom Van Brunt, the hero of the country round, which rang with his feats of strength and hardihood. He was broad-shouldered and double-jointed, with short curly black hair, and a bluff, but not unpleasant countenance, having a mingled air of fun and arrogance. From his Herculean frame and great powers of limb, he had received the nickname of BROM BONES, by which he was universally known. He was famed for great knowledge and skill in horsemanship, being as dexterous on horseback as a Tartar. He was foremost at all races and cock-fights; and, with the ascendency which bodily strength acquires in rustic life, was the umpire in all disputes, setting his hat on one side, and giving his decisions with an air and tone admitting of no gainsay or appeal. He was always ready for either a fight or a frolic; but had more mischief than ill-will in his composition; and, with all his overbearing roughness, there was a strong dash of waggish good humor at bottom. He had three or four boon companions, who regarded him as their model, and at the head of whom he scoured the country, attending every scene of feud or merriment for miles round. In cold weather he was distinguished by a fur cap, surmounted with a flaunting fox's tail; and when the folks at a country gathering descried this well-known crest at a distance, whisking about among a squad of hard riders, they always stood by for a squall. Sometimes his crew would be heard dashing along past the farmhouses at midnight, with whoop and halloo, like a troop of Don Cossacks; and the old dames, startled out of their sleep, would listen for a moment till the hurry-scurry had clattered by, and then exclaim, "Ay, there goes Brom Bones and his gang!" The neighbors looked upon him with a mixture of awe, admiration, and good will; and when any madcap prank, or rustic brawl, occurred in the vicinity, always shook their heads, and warranted Brom Bones was at the bottom of it.

This rantipole[24] hero had for some time singled out the blooming Katrina for the object of his uncouth gallantries, and though his amorous toyings were something like the gentle caresses and endearments of a bear, yet it was whispered that she did not altogether discourage his hopes. Certain it is, his advances were signals for rival candidates to retire, who felt no inclination to cross a lion in his amours;[25] insomuch, that when his horse was seen tied to Van Tassel's paling, on a Sunday night, a sure sign that his master was courting, or, as it is termed, "sparking," within, all other suitors passed by in despair, and carried the war into other quarters.

Such was the formidable rival with whom Ichabod Crane had to contend, and, considering all things, a stouter man than he would have shrunk from the competition, and a wiser man would have despaired. He had, however, a happy mixture of pliability and perseverance in his nature; he was in form and spirit like a supple-jack—yielding, but tough; though he bent, he never broke: and though he bowed beneath the slightest pressure, yet, the moment it was away—jerk! he was as erect, and carried his head as high as ever. To have taken the field openly against his rival would have been madness; for he was not a man to be thwarted in his amours, any more than that stormy lover, Achilles. Ichabod, therefore, made his advances in a quiet and gently-insinuating manner. Under cover of his character of singing-master, he made frequent visits at the farmhouse; not that he had any thing to apprehend from the meddlesome interference of parents, which is so often a stumbling-block in the path of lovers. Balt Van Tassel was an easy indulgent soul; he loved his daughter better even than his pipe, and, like a reasonable man and an excellent father, let her have her way in every thing. His notable little wife, too, had enough to do to attend to her housekeeping and manage her poultry; for, as she sagely observed, ducks

---

[24] Wild.
[25] Love.

and geese are foolish things, and must be looked after, but girls can take care of themselves. Thus while the busy dame bustled about the house, or plied her spinning-wheel at one end of the piazza, honest Balt would sit smoking his evening pipe at the other, watching the achievements of a little wooden warrior, who, armed with a sword in each hand, was most valiantly fighting the wind on the pinnacle of the barn. In the mean time, Ichabod would carry on his suit with the daughter by the side of the spring under the great elm, or sauntering along in the twilight, that hour so favorable to the lover's eloquence.

I profess not to know how women's hearts are wooed and won. To me they have always been matters of riddle and admiration. Some seem to have but one vulnerable point, or door of access; while others have a thousand avenues, and may be captured in a thousand different ways. It is a great triumph of skill to gain the former, but a still greater proof of generalship to maintain possession of the latter, for the man must battle for his fortress at every door and window. He who wins a thousand common hearts is therefore entitled to some renown; but he who keeps undisputed sway over the heart of a coquette, is indeed a hero. Certain it is, this was not the case with the redoubtable Brom Bones; and from the moment Ichabod Crane made his advances, the interests of the former evidently declined; his horse was no longer seen tied at the palings on Sunday nights, and a deadly feud gradually arose between him and the preceptor[26] of Sleepy Hollow. Brom, who had a degree of rough chivalry in his nature, would fain have carried matters to open warfare, and have settled their pretensions to the lady, according to the mode of those most concise and simple reasoners, the knights-errant of yore—by single combat; but Ichabod was too conscious of the superior might of his adversary to enter the lists against him: he had overheard a boast of Bones, that he would "double the

---

[26] Teacher.

schoolmaster up, and lay him on a shelf of his own school-house;" and he was too wary to give him an opportunity. There was something extremely provoking in this obstinately pacific system; it left Brom no alternative but to draw upon the funds of rustic waggery in his disposition, and to play off boorish practical jokes upon his rival. Ichabod became the object of whimsical persecution to Bones, and his gang of rough riders. They harried his hitherto peaceful domains; smoked out his singing school, by stopping up the chimney; broke into the school-house at night, in spite of its formidable fastenings of withe and window stakes, and turned every thing topsy-turvy: so that the poor schoolmaster began to think all the witches in the country held their meetings there. But what was still more annoying, Brom took all opportunities of turning him into ridicule in presence of his mistress, and had a scoundrel dog whom he taught to whine in the most ludicrous manner, and introduced as a rival of Ichabod's to instruct her in psalmody.

In this way matters went on for some time, without producing any material effect on the relative situation of the contending powers. On a fine autumnal afternoon, Ichabod, in pensive mood, sat enthroned on the lofty stool whence he usually watched all the concerns of his little literary realm. In his hand he swayed a ferule,[27] that sceptre of despotic power; the birch of justice reposed on three nails, behind the throne, a constant terror to evil doers; while on the desk before him might be seen sundry contraband articles and prohibited weapons, detected upon the persons of idle urchins; such as half-munched apples, popguns, whirligigs, fly-cages, and whole legions of rampant little paper game-cocks. Apparently there had been some appalling act of justice recently inflicted, for his scholars were all busily intent upon their books, or slyly whispering behind them with one eye kept upon the

---

[27] Rod, cane, or flat ruler, often used for punishment; in Crane's case, it appears he keeps the "birch of justice" on display for special occasions, in contrast to the ferule, which he carries about the school-house.

master; and a kind of buzzing stillness reigned throughout the school-room. It was suddenly interrupted by the appearance of a negro, in tow-cloth jacket and trowsers, a round-crowned fragment of a hat, like the cap of Mercury, and mounted on the back of a ragged, wild, half-broken colt, which he managed with a rope by way of halter. He came clattering up to the school door with an invitation to Ichabod to attend a merry-making or "quilting frolic,"[28] to be held that evening at Mynheer[29] Van Tassel's; and having delivered his message with that air of importance, and effort at fine language, which a negro is apt to display on petty embassies of the kind, he dashed over the brook, and was seen scampering away up the hollow, full of the importance and hurry of his mission.

All was now bustle and hubbub in the late quiet school-room. The scholars were hurried through their lessons, without stopping at trifles; those who were nimble skipped over half with impunity, and those who were tardy, had a smart application now and then in the rear, to quicken their speed, or help them over a tall word. Books were flung aside without being put away on the shelves, inkstands were over-turned, benches thrown down, and the whole school was turned loose an hour before the usual time, bursting forth like a legion of young imps, yelping and racketing about the green, in joy at their early emancipation.

The gallant Ichabod now spent at least an extra half hour at his toilet, brushing and furbishing up his best, and indeed only suit of rusty black, and arranging his looks by a bit of broken looking-glass, that hung up in the school-house. That he might make his appearance before his mistress in the true style of a cavalier, he borrowed a horse from the farmer with whom he was domiciliated,[30] a choleric[31] old Dutchman, of

---

[28] Quilting Bee; guests assist in quilting while music is played and food is enjoyed. A dance follows.

[29] The equivalent of "mister," or a title of respect. From Dutch *myn*="my" and *heer*="lord."

[30] Staying in the house of.

[31] Grumpy or irritable.

the name of Hans Van Ripper, and, thus gallantly mounted, issued forth, like a knight-errant in quest of adventures. But it is meet I should, in the true spirit of romantic story, give some account of the looks and equipments of my hero and his steed. The animal he bestrode was a broken-down plough-horse, that had outlived almost every thing but his viciousness. He was gaunt and shagged, with a ewe neck and a head like a hammer; his rusty mane and tail were tangled and knotted with burrs; one eye had lost its pupil, and was glaring and spectral; but the other had the gleam of a genuine devil in it. Still he must have had fire and mettle in his day, if we may judge from the name he bore of Gunpowder. He had, in fact, been a favorite steed of his master's, the choleric Van Ripper, who was a furious rider, and had infused, very probably, some of his own spirit into the animal; for, old and broken-down as he looked, there was more of the lurking devil in him than in any young filly in the country.

Ichabod was a suitable figure for such a steed. He rode with short stirrups, which brought his knees nearly up to the pommel of the saddle; his sharp elbows stuck out like grass-hoppers'; he carried his whip perpendicularly in his hand, like a sceptre, and, as his horse jogged on, the motion of his arms was not unlike the flapping of a pair of wings. A small wool hat rested on the top of his nose, for so his scanty strip of forehead might be called; and the skirts of his black coat fluttered out almost to the horse's tail. Such was the appearance of Ichabod and his steed, as they shambled out of the gate of Hans Van Ripper, and it was altogether such an apparition as is seldom to be met with in broad daylight.

It was, as I have said, a fine autumnal day, the sky was clear and serene, and nature wore that rich and golden livery which we always associate with the idea of abundance. The forests had put on their sober brown and yellow, while some trees of the tenderer kind had been nipped by the frosts into brilliant dyes of orange, purple, and scarlet. Streaming files of wild ducks began to make their appearance high in the air; the bark of the squirrel might be heard from the groves of beech and hickory nuts, and the pensive whistle of the quail at intervals from the neighboring stubble-field.

The small birds were taking their farewell banquets. In the fulness of their revelry, they fluttered, chirping and frolicking, from bush to bush, and tree to tree, capricious from the very profusion and variety around them. There was the honest cock-robin, the favorite game of stripling sportsmen, with its loud querulous[32] note; and the twittering blackbirds flying in sable clouds; and the golden-winged woodpecker, with his crimson crest, his broad black gorget,[33] and splendid plumage; and the cedar bird, with its red-tipt wings and yellow-tipt tail, and its little monteiro[34] cap of feathers; and the blue-jay, that noisy coxcomb, in his gay light-blue coat and white under-clothes; screaming and chattering, nodding and bobbing and bowing, and pretending to be on good terms with every songster of the grove.

As Ichabod jogged slowly on his way, his eye, ever open to every symptom of culinary abundance, ranged with delight over the treasures of jolly autumn. On all sides he beheld vast store of apples; some hanging in oppressive opulence on the trees; some gathered into baskets and barrels for the market; others heaped up in rich piles for the cider-press. Farther on he beheld great fields of Indian corn, with its golden ears peeping from their leafy coverts, and holding out the promise of cakes and hasty pudding; and the yellow pumpkins lying beneath them, turning up their fair round bellies to the sun, and giving ample prospects of the most luxurious of pies; and anon he passed the fragrant buckwheat fields, breathing the odor of the bee-hive, and as he beheld them, soft anticipations stole over his mind of dainty slapjacks, well buttered, and garnished with honey or treacle, by the delicate little dimpled hand of Katrina Van Tassel.

---

[32] Whining.
[33] Throat.
[34] Hunting cap.

Thus feeding his mind with many sweet thoughts and "sugared suppositions," he journeyed along the sides of a range of hills which look out upon some of the goodliest scenes of the mighty Hudson. The sun gradually wheeled his broad disk down into the west. The wide bosom of the Tappan Zee lay motionless and glassy, excepting that here and there a gentle undulation waved and prolonged the blue shadow of the distant mountain. A few amber clouds floated in the sky, without a breath of air to move them. The horizon was of a fine golden tint, changing gradually into a pure apple green, and from that into the deep blue of the mid-heaven. A slanting ray lingered on the woody crests of the precipices that overhung some parts of the river, giving greater depth to the dark-gray and purple of their rocky sides. A sloop was loitering in the distance, dropping slowly down with the tide, her sail hanging uselessly against the mast; and as the reflection of the sky gleamed along the still water, it seemed as if the vessel was suspended in the air.

It was toward evening that Ichabod arrived at the castle of the Heer Van Tassel, which he found thronged with the pride and flower of the adjacent country. Old farmers, a spare leathern-faced race, in homespun coats and breeches blue stockings, huge shoes, and magnificent pewter buckles. Their brisk, withered little dames, in close crimped caps, long waisted short-gowns, homespun petticoats, with scissors and pincushions, and gay calico pockets hanging on the outside.[35] Buxom lasses, almost as antiquated as their mothers, excepting where a straw hat, a fine ribbon, or perhaps a white frock, gave symptoms of city innovation. The sons, in short square-skirted coats with rows of stupendous brass buttons, and their hair generally queued in the fashion of the times, especially if they could procure an eel-skin for the purpose, it being esteemed, throughout the country, as a potent nourisher and strengthener of the hair.

---

[35] Scissors, pincushions, and calico pockets remind the reader that this is a "quilting frolic."

Brom Bones, however, was the hero of the scene, having come to the gathering on his favorite steed Daredevil, a creature, like himself, full of mettle and mischief, and which no one but himself could manage. He was, in fact, noted for preferring vicious animals, given to all kinds of tricks, which kept the rider in constant risk of his neck, for he held a tractable[36] well-broken horse as unworthy of a lad of spirit.

Fain would I pause to dwell upon the world of charms that burst upon the enraptured gaze of my hero, as he entered the state parlor of Van Tassel's mansion. Not those of the bevy of buxom lasses, with their luxurious display of red and white; but the ample charms of a genuine Dutch country tea-table, in the sumptuous time of autumn. Such heaped-up platters of cakes of various and almost indescribable kinds, known only to experienced Dutch housewives! There was the doughty dough-nut, the tenderer oly koek, and the crisp and crumbling cruller; sweet cakes and short cakes, ginger cakes and honey cakes, and the whole family of cakes. And then there were apple pies and peach pies and pumpkin pies; besides slices of ham and smoked beef; and moreover delectable dishes of preserved plums, and peaches, and pears, and quinces; not to mention broiled shad and roasted chickens; together with bowls of milk and cream, all mingled higgledy-piggledy, pretty much as I have enumerated them, with the motherly tea-pot sending up its clouds of vapor from the midst—Heaven bless the mark! I want breath and time to discuss this banquet as it deserves, and am too eager to get on with my story. Happily, Ichabod Crane was not in so great a hurry as his historian, but did ample justice to every dainty.

He was a kind and thankful creature, whose heart dilated in proportion as his skin was filled with good cheer; and whose spirits rose with eating as some men's do with drink. He could not help, too, rolling his large eyes round him as he ate, and chuckling with the possibility that he might one day be lord of

---

[36] Easy to manage.

all this scene of almost unimaginable luxury and splendor. Then, he thought, how soon he'd turn his back upon the old school-house; snap his fingers in the face of Hans Van Ripper, and every other niggardly patron, and kick any itinerant pedagogue out of doors that should dare to call him comrade.

Old Baltus Van Tassel moved about among his guests with a face dilated with content and good humor, round and jolly as the harvest moon. His hospitable attentions were brief, but expressive, being confined to a shake of the hand, a slap on the shoulder, a loud laugh, and a pressing invitation to "fall to, and help themselves."

And now the sound of the music from the common room, or hall, summoned to the dance. The musician was an old grayheaded negro, who had been the itinerant orchestra of the neighborhood for more than half a century. His instrument was as old and battered as himself. The greater part of the time he scraped on two or three strings, accompanying every movement of the bow with a motion of the head; bowing almost of the ground, and stamping with his foot whenever a fresh couple were to start.

Ichabod prided himself upon his dancing as much as upon his vocal powers. Not a limb, not a fibre about him was idle, and to have seen his loosely hung frame in full motion, and clattering about the room, you would have thought Saint Vitus himself, that blessed patron of the dance, was figuring before you in person. He was the admiration of all the negroes; who, having gathered, of all ages and sizes, from the farm and the neighborhood, stood forming a pyramid of shining black faces at every door and window, gazing with delight at the scene, rolling their white eye-balls, and showing grinning rows of ivory from ear to ear. How could the flogger of urchins be otherwise than animated and joyous? The lady of his heart was his partner in the dance, and smiling graciously in reply to all his amorous oglings; while Brom Bones, sorely smitten with love and jealousy, sat brooding by himself in one corner.

When the dance was at an end, Ichabod was attracted to a knot of the sager folks, who, with old Van Tassel, sat smoking at one end of the piazza, gossiping over former times, and drawing out long stories about the war.

This neighborhood, at the time of which I am speaking, was one of those highly-favored places which abound with chronicle and great men. The British and American line had run near it during the war; it had, therefore, been the scene of marauding, and infested with refugees, cow-boys, and all kinds of border chivalry. Just sufficient time had elapsed to enable each story-teller to dress up his tale with a little becoming fiction, and, in the indistinctness of his recollection, to make himself the hero of every exploit.

There was the story of Doffue Martling, a large blue beard-ed Dutchman, who had nearly taken a British frigate with an old iron nine-pounder from a mud breastwork, only that his gun burst at the sixth discharge. And there was an old gentleman who shall be nameless, being too rich a mynheer to be lightly mentioned, who, in the battle of Whiteplains, being an excellent master of defence, parried a musket-ball with a small sword, insomuch that he absolutely felt it whiz round the blade, and glance off at the hilt: in proof of which, he was ready at any time to show the sword, with the hilt a little bent. There were several more that had been equally great in the field, not one of whom but was persuaded that he had a considerable hand in bringing the war to a happy termination.

But all these were nothing to the tales of ghosts and apparitions that succeeded. The neighborhood is rich in legendary treasures of the kind. Local tales and superstitions thrive best in these sheltered long-settled retreats; but are trampled under foot by the shifting throng that forms the population of most of our country places. Besides, there is no encouragement for ghosts in most of our villages, for they have scarcely had time to finish their first nap, and turn themselves in their graves, before their surviving friends have travelled away from the neighborhood; so that when they turn out at night to walk their rounds, they have no acquaintance left to call upon. This is perhaps the reason why we so seldom hear of ghosts except in our long-established Dutch communities.

The immediate cause, however, of the prevalence of supernatural stories in these parts, was doubtless owing to the vicinity of Sleepy Hollow. There was a contagion in the very air that blew from that haunted region; it breathed forth an atmosphere of dreams and fancies infecting all the land. Several of the Sleepy Hollow people were present at Van Tassel's, and, as usual, were doling out their wild and wonderful legends. Many dismal tales were told about funeral trains, and mourning cries and wailings heard and seen about the great tree where the unfortunate Major André was taken, and which stood in the neighborhood.[37] Some mention was made also of the woman in white, that haunted the dark glen at Raven Rock, and was often heard to shriek on winter nights before a storm, having perished there in the snow. The chief part of the stories, however, turned upon the favorite spectre of Sleepy Hollow, the headless horseman, who had been heard several times of late, patrolling the country; and, it was said, tethered his horse nightly among the graves in the church-yard.

The sequestered situation of this church seems always to have made it a favorite haunt of troubled spirits. It stands on a knoll, surrounded by locust-trees and lofty elms, from among which its decent whitewashed walls shine modestly forth, like Christian purity beaming through the shades of retirement. A gentle slope descends from it to a silver sheet of water, bordered by high trees, between which, peeps may be caught at the blue hills of the Hudson. To look upon its grass-grown yard, where the sunbeams seem to sleep so quietly, one would think that there at least the dead might rest in peace. On one side of the church extends a wide woody dell, along which

---

[37] Major André was a British Officer hanged as a spy for his role in subverting Benedict Arnold, although Irving infers that Sleepy Hollow and Tarry Town folk were sympathetic to André.

raves a large brook among broken rocks and trunks of fallen trees. Over a deep black part of the stream, not far from the church, was formerly thrown a wooden bridge; the road that led to it, and the bridge itself, were thickly shaded by over-hanging trees, which cast a gloom about it, even in the day-time; but occasioned a fearful darkness at night. This was one of the favorite haunts of the headless horseman; and the place where he was most frequently encountered. The tale was told of old Brouwer, a most heretical disbeliever in ghosts, how he met the horseman returning from his foray into Sleepy Hol-low, and was obliged to get up behind him; how they galloped over bush and brake, over hill and swamp, until they reached the bridge; when the horseman suddenly turned into a skele-ton, threw old Brouwer into the brook, and sprang away over the tree-tops with a clap of thunder.

This story was immediately matched by a thrice marvellous adventure of Brom Bones, who made light of the galloping Hessian as an arrant jockey. He affirmed that, on returning one night from the neighboring village of Sing Sing, he had been overtaken by this midnight trooper; that he had offered to race with him for a bowl of punch, and should have won it too, for Daredevil beat the goblin horse all hollow, but, just as they came to the church bridge, the Hessian bolted, and vanished in a flash of fire.

All these tales, told in that drowsy undertone with which men talk in the dark, the countenances of the listeners only now and then receiving a casual gleam from the glare of a pipe, sank deep in the mind of Ichabod. He repaid them in kind with large extracts from his invaluable author, Cotton Mather, and added many marvellous events that had taken place in his native State of Connecticut, and fearful sights which he had seen in his nightly walks about Sleepy Hollow.

The revel now gradually broke up. The old farmers gath-ered together their families in their wagons, and were heard for some time rattling along the hollow roads, and over the distant hills. Some of the damsels mounted on pillions[38] behind their favorite swains,[39] and their light-hearted laughter, mingling with the clatter of hoofs, echoed along the silent wood-lands, sounding fainter and fainter until they gradually died away—and the late scene of noise and frolic was all silent and deserted. Ichabod only lingered behind, according to the custom of country lovers, to have a tête-à-tête[40] with the heiress, fully convinced that he was now on the high road to success. What passed at this interview I will not pretend to say, for in fact I do not know. Something, however, I fear me, must have gone wrong, for he certainly sallied forth, after no very great interval, with an air quite desolate and chop-fallen.—Oh these women! these women! Could that girl have been playing off any of her coquettish tricks?—Was her encouragement of the poor pedagogue all a mere sham to secure her conquest of his rival?—Heaven only knows, not I!—Let it suffice to say, Ichabod stole forth with the air of one who had been sacking a hen-roost, rather than a fair lady's heart. Without looking to the right or left to notice the scene of rural wealth, on which he had so often gloated, he went straight to the stable, and with several hearty cuffs and kicks, roused his steed most uncourteously from the comfortable quarters in which he was soundly sleeping, dreaming of mountains of corn and oats, and whole valleys of timothy and clover.

It was the very witching time of night that Ichabod, heavy-hearted and crest-fallen, pursued his travel homewards, along the sides of the lofty hills which rise above Tarry Town, and which he had traversed so cheerily in the afternoon. The hour was as dismal as himself. Far below him, the Tappan Zee spread its dusky and indistinct waste of waters, with here and there the tall mast of a sloop, riding quietly at anchor under the land. In the dead hush of midnight, he could even hear the

---

[38] Cushion attached behind a saddle for an extra rider.
[39] A country boy; also, a young sweetheart.
[40] Private conversation between two people.

barking of the watch dog from the opposite shore of the Hudson; but it was so vague and faint as only to give an idea of his distance from this faithful companion of man. Now and then, too, the long-drawn crowing of a cock, accidentally awakened, would sound far, far off, from some farm-house away among the hills—but it was like a dreaming sound in his ear. No signs of life occurred near him, but occasionally the melancholy chirp of a cricket, or perhaps the guttural twang of a bull-frog, from a neighboring marsh, as if sleeping un-comfortably, and turning suddenly in his bed.

All the stories of ghosts and goblins that he had heard in the afternoon, now came crowding upon his recollection. The night grew darker and darker; the stars seemed to sink deeper in the sky, and driving clouds occasionally hid them from his sight. He had never felt so lonely and dismal. He was, moreo-ver, approaching the very place where many of the scenes of the ghost stories had been laid. In the centre of the road stood an enormous tulip-tree, which towered like a giant above all the other trees of the neighborhood, and formed a kind of landmark. Its limbs were gnarled, and fantastic, large enough to form trunks for ordinary trees, twisting down almost to the earth, and rising again into the air. It was connected with the tragical story of the unfortunate André, who had been taken prisoner hard by; and was universally known by the name of Major André's tree. The common people regarded it with a mixture of respect and superstition, partly out of sympathy for the fate of its ill-starred namesake, and partly from the tales of strange sights and doleful lamentations told concern-ing it.

As Ichabod approached this fearful tree, he began to whis-tle: he thought his whistle was answered—it was but a blast sweeping sharply through the dry branches. As he approached a little nearer, he thought he saw something white, hanging in the midst of the tree—he paused and ceased whistling; but on looking more narrowly, perceived that it was a place where the tree had been scathed by lightning, and the white wood laid bare. Suddenly he heard a groan—his teeth chattered and his knees smote against the saddle: it was but the rubbing of one huge bough upon another, as they were swayed about by the breeze. He passed the tree in safety, but new perils lay before him.

About two hundred yards from the tree a small brook crossed the road, and ran into a marshy and thickly-wooded glen, known by the name of Wiley's swamp. A few rough logs, laid side by side, served for a bridge over this stream. On that side of the road where the brook entered the wood, a group of oaks and chestnuts, matted thick with wild grape-vines, threw a cavernous gloom over it. To pass this bridge was the severest trial. It was at this identical spot that the unfortunate André was captured, and under the covert of those chestnuts and vines were the sturdy yeomen concealed who surprised him. This has ever since been considered a haunted stream, and fearful are the feelings of the schoolboy who has to pass it alone after dark.

As he approached the stream his heart began to thump; he summoned up, however, all his resolution, gave his horse half a score of kicks in the ribs, and attempted to dash briskly across the bridge; but instead of starting forward, the perverse old animal made a lateral movement, and ran broadside against the fence. Ichabod, whose fears increased with the delay, jerked the reins on the other side, and kicked lustily with the contrary foot: it was all in vain; his steed started, it is true, but it was only to plunge to the opposite side of the road into a thicket of brambles and alder bushes. The schoolmaster now bestowed both whip and heel upon the starveling[41] ribs of old Gunpowder, who dashed forward, snuffling and snorting, but came to a stand just by the bridge, with a suddenness that had nearly sent his rider sprawling over his head. Just at this moment a plashy tramp by the side of the bridge caught the sensitive ear of Ichabod. In the dark shadow of the grove,

---

[41] Lacking food; emaciated.

on the margin of the brook, he beheld something huge, mis-shapen, black and towering. It stirred not, but seemed gathered up in the gloom, like some gigantic monster ready to spring upon the traveller.

The hair of the affrighted pedagogue rose upon his head with terror. What was to be done? To turn and fly was now too late; and besides, what chance was there of escaping ghost or goblin, if such it was, which could ride upon the wings of the wind? Summoning up, therefore, a show of courage, he demanded in stammering accents—"Who are you?" He received no reply. He repeated his demand in a still more agitated voice. Still there was no answer. Once more he cudgelled the sides of the inflexible Gunpowder, and, shutting his eyes, broke forth with involuntary fervor into a psalm tune. Just then the shadowy object of alarm put itself in motion, and, with a scramble and a bound, stood at once in the middle of the road. Though the night was dark and dismal, yet the form of the unknown might now in some degree be ascertained. He appeared to be a horseman of large dimensions, and mounted on a black horse of powerful frame. He made no offer of molestation or sociability, but kept aloof on one side of the road, jogging along on the blind side of old Gunpowder, who had now got over his fright and waywardness.

Ichabod, who had no relish for this strange midnight companion, and bethought himself of the adventure of Brom Bones with the Galloping Hessian, now quickened his steed, in hopes of leaving him behind. The stranger, however, quickened his horse to an equal pace. Ichabod pulled up and fell into a walk, thinking to lag behind—the other did the same. His heart began to sink within him; he endeavored to resume his psalm tune, but his parched tongue clove to the roof of his mouth, and he could not utter a stave. There was something in the moody and dogged silence of this pertinacious[42] companion, that was mysterious and appalling. It was soon fearfully accounted for. On mounting a rising ground, which brought the figure of his fellow-traveller in relief against the sky, gigantic in height, and muffled in a cloak, Ichabod was horror-struck, on perceiving that he was headless!—but his horror was still more increased, on observing that the head, which should have rested on his shoulders, was carried before him on the pommel of the saddle: his terror rose to desperation; he rained a shower of kicks and blows upon Gunpowder, hoping, by a sudden movement, to give his companion the slip—but the spectre started full jump with him. Away then they dashed, through thick and thin; stones flying, and sparks flashing at every bound. Ichabod's flimsy garments fluttered in the air, as he stretched his long lank body away over his horse's head, in the eagerness of his flight.

They had now reached the road which turns off to Sleepy Hollow; but Gunpowder, who seemed possessed with a demon, instead of keeping up it, made an opposite turn, and plunged headlong down hill to the left. This road leads through a sandy hollow, shaded by trees for about a quarter of a mile, where it crosses the bridge famous in goblin story, and just beyond swells the green knoll on which stands the white-washed church.

As yet the panic of the steed had given his unskilful rider an apparent advantage in the chase; but just as he had got half way through the hollow, the girths of the saddle gave way, and he felt it slipping from under him. He seized it by the pommel, and endeavored to hold it firm, but in vain; and had just time to save himself by clasping old Gunpowder round the neck, when the saddle fell to the earth, and he heard it trampled under foot by his pursuer. For a moment the terror of Hans Van Ripper's wrath passed across his mind—for it was his Sunday saddle; but this was no time for petty fears; the goblin was hard on his haunches; and (unskilful rider that he was!)

---

[42] Unreasonably stubborn.

he had much ado to maintain his seat; sometimes slipping on one side, sometimes on another, and sometimes jolted on the high ridge of his horse's back-bone, with a violence that he verily feared would cleave him asunder.

An opening in the trees now cheered him with the hopes that the church bridge was at hand. The wavering reflection of a silver star in the bosom of the brook told him that he was not mistaken. He saw the walls of the church dimly glaring under the trees beyond. He recollected the place where Brom Bones's ghostly competitor had disappeared. "If I can but reach that bridge," thought Ichabod, "I am safe." Just then he heard the black steed panting and blowing close behind him; he even fancied that he felt his hot breath. Another convulsive kick in the ribs, and old Gunpowder sprang upon the bridge; he thundered over the resounding planks; he gained the opposite side; and now Ichabod cast a look behind to see if his pursuer should vanish, according to rule, in a flash of fire and brimstone. Just then he saw the goblin rising in his stirrups, and in the very act of hurling his head at him, Ichabod endeavored to dodge the horrible missile, but too late. It encountered his cranium with a tremendous crash—he was tumbled headlong into the dust, and Gunpowder, the black steed, and the goblin rider, passed by like a whirlwind.

The next morning the old horse was found without his saddle, and with the bridle under his feet, soberly cropping the grass at his master's gate. Ichabod did not make his appearance at breakfast; dinner-hour came, but no Ichabod. The boys assembled at the school-house, and strolled idly about the banks of the brook; but no school-master. Hans Van Ripper now began to feel some uneasiness about the fate of poor Ichabod, and his saddle. An inquiry was set on foot, and after diligent investigation they came upon his traces. In one part of the road leading to the church was found the saddle trampled in the dirt; the tracks of horses' hoofs deeply dented in the road, and evidently at furious speed, were traced to the bridge, beyond which, on the bank of a broad part of the brook, where the water ran deep and black, was found the hat of the unfortunate Ichabod, and close beside it a shattered pumpkin.

The brook was searched, but the body of the school-master was not to be discovered. Hans Van Ripper, as executor of his estate, examined the bundle which contained all his worldly effects. They consisted of two shirts and a half; two stocks for the neck; a pair or two of worsted stockings; an old pair of corduroy small-clothes;[43] a rusty razor; a book of psalm tunes, full of dogs' ears; and a broken pitchpipe. As to the books and furniture of the school-house, they belonged to the community, excepting Cotton Mather's History of Witchcraft, a New England Almanac, and a book of dreams and fortune-telling; in which last was a sheet of foolscap much scribbled and blotted in several fruitless attempts to make a copy of verses in honor of the heiress of Van Tassel. These magic books and the poetic scrawl were forthwith consigned to the flames by Hans Van Ripper; who from that time forward determined to send his children no more to school; observing, that he never knew any good come of this same reading and writing. Whatever money the schoolmaster possessed, and he had received his quarter's pay but a day or two before, he must have had about his person at the time of his disappearance.

The mysterious event caused much speculation at the church on the following Sunday. Knots of gazers and gossips were collected in the church-yard, at the bridge, and at the spot where the hat and pumpkin had been found. The stories of Brouwer, of Bones, and a whole budget of others, were called to mind; and when they had diligently considered them all, and compared them with the symptoms of the present case, they shook their heads, and came to the conclusion that Ichabod had been carried off by the galloping Hessian. As he was a bachelor, and in nobody's debt, nobody troubled his head any more about him. The school was removed to a

---

[43] Knee-breeches; probably used as underwear.

different quarter of the hollow, and another pedagogue reigned in his stead.

It is true, an old farmer, who had been down to New York on a visit several years after, and from whom this account of the ghostly adventure was received, brought home the intelligence that Ichabod Crane was still alive; that he had left the neighborhood, partly through fear of the goblin and Hans Van Ripper, and partly in mortification at having been suddenly dismissed by the heiress; that he had changed his quarters to a distant part of the country; had kept school and studied law at the same time, had been admitted to the bar, turned politician, electioneered, written for the newspapers, and finally had been made a justice of the Ten Pound Court. Brom Bones too, who shortly after his rival's disappearance conducted the blooming Katrina in triumph to the altar, was observed to look exceedingly knowing whenever the story of Ichabod was related, and always burst into a hearty laugh at the mention of the pumpkin; which led some to suspect that he knew more about the matter than he chose to tell.

The old country wives, however, who are the best judges of these matters, maintain to this day that Ichabod was spirited away by supernatural means; and it is a favorite story often told about the neighborhood round the winter evening fire. The bridge became more than ever an object of superstitious awe, and that may be the reason why the road has been altered of late years, so as to approach the church by the border of the mill-pond. The school-house being deserted, soon fell to decay, and was reported to be haunted by the ghost of the unfortunate pedagogue; and the ploughboy, loitering homeward of a still summer evening, has often fancied his voice at a distance, chanting a melancholy psalm tune among the tranquil solitudes of Sleepy Hollow.

POSTSCRIPT
FOUND IN THE HANDWRITING OF MR. KNICKER-
BOCKER.

THE preceding Tale is given, almost in the precise words in which I heard it related at a Corporation meeting of the ancient city of Manhattoes, at which were present many of its sagest and most illustrious burghers.[44] The narrator was a pleasant, shabby, gentlemanly old fellow, in pepper-and-salt clothes, with a sadly humorous face; and one whom I strongly suspected of being poor, he made such efforts to be entertaining. When his story was concluded, there was much laughter and approbation,[45] particularly from two or three deputy aldermen, who had been asleep a greater part of the time. There was, however, one tall, dry-looking old gentleman, with beetling eyebrows, who maintained a grave and rather severe face throughout: now and then folding his arms, inclining his head, and looking down upon the floor, as if turning a doubt over in his mind. He was one of your wary men, who never laugh, but upon good grounds—when they have reason and the law on their side. When the mirth of the rest of the company had subsided, and silence was restored, he leaned one arm on the elbow of his chair, and, sticking the other akimbo, demanded, with a slight but exceedingly sage motion of the head, and contraction of the brow, what was the moral of the story, and what it went to prove?

The story-teller, who was just putting a glass of wine to his lips, as a refreshment after his toils, paused for a moment, looked at his inquirer with an air of infinite deference, and, lowering the glass slowly to the table, observed, that the story was intended most logically to prove:—

"That there is no situation in life but has its advantages and pleasures,—provided we will but take a joke as we find it;

---

[44] A citizen, esp. one who is wealthy or elite.
[45] Approval.

"That, therefore, he that runs races with goblin troopers is likely to have rough riding of it.

"Ergo, for a country schoolmaster to be refused the hand of a Dutch heiress, is a certain step to high preferment in the state."

The cautious old gentleman knit his brows tenfold closer after this explanation, being sorely puzzled by the ratiocination[46] of the syllogism;[47] while, methought, the one in pepper-and-salt eyed him with something of a triumphant leer. At length, he observed, that all this was very well, but still he thought the story a little on the extravagant—there were one or two points on which he had his doubts. "Faith, sir," replied the story-teller, "as to that matter, I don't believe one-half of it myself."

D. K.

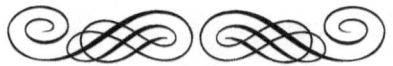

---

[46] Reasoning.
[47] Process of deducing.

AFTERWORD

The Legend of Sleepy Hollow was published in 1820 in the second volume of a collection of loosely-related essays titled *The Sketch Book of Geoffrey Crayon, Gent.* Although written by Washington Irving, the "sketches" of the book were presented from the pen of the fictional Geoffrey Crayon.

Eleven years before *The Sketch Book*, Irving published *Knickerbocker's History of New York*. Irving presented this earlier book as a collection of writings of another fictional character, the Dutch historian Diedrich Knickerbocker.

The Legend of Sleepy Hollow, as one of the final stories in *The Sketch Book*, connects both Irving's fictional narrators. Immediately beneath the title is the note "Found Among the Papers of the Late Diedrich Knickerbocker." In the post script to the legend, Knickerbocker tells his readers that he wrote "almost the precise words" of the original story as he heard it at "a Corporation meeting of the ancient city of Manhattoes."

Following this literary labyrinth, an unnamed narrator told *The Legend of Sleepy Hollow* to Diedrich Knickerbocker, who recorded it; it was then collected among the sketches of Geoffrey Crayon. Yet neither Knickerbocker or Crayon exist; both are the inventions of Washington Irving. We have Irving's version of the telephone game: a story that is passed from one ear to another ear to another ear and then, finally, to us.

The construction of *The Legend of Sleepy Hollow* is completely different from the expectations of a contemporary reader. Today's fiction hits the action as quickly as possible; eliminates exposition; moves the story with the rapid exchange of dialogue, which fills in for exposition by providing characterization. *Sleepy Hollow* does none of these things.

Irving writes nearly 5,700 words before he finally hits the first moment of actual narrative story: "On a fine autumnal afternoon, Ichabod, in pensive mood, sat enthroned on the

93

lofty stool..." Everything before this moment explains: explains the area surrounding Sleepy Hollow, explains the history of the Horseman, explains Ichabod's personality, explains the affection he has for Katrina Van Tassel's inheritance, explains the conflict between Ichabod and Brom Bones for the heiress, explains, explains, explains...

For dialogue, Irving summarizes; he rarely records a character's spoken words. When Brom Bones and his gang race around the country-side late at night, the "old dames...exclaim, 'Ay, there goes Brom Bones and his gang.'" This isn't a single speaker, but a generic speech spoken many times in many places when the gang is heard. Baltus Van Tassel tells his guests: "'fall to, and help themselves,'" which is still a summary since a speaker would not use the third person "themselves"; instead, he would have said, "yourselves." In the post script, Irving uses the vehicle of dialogue for three possible lessons that could be learned from the story. The narrator concludes the legend by explaining (in dialogue) "'Faith, sir' replied the story-teller, 'as to that matter, I don't believe one-half of it myself.'" In no instance does Irving have characters involved in back-and-forth conversation using dialogue. The closest he comes is when Ichabod Crane briefly confronts the dark horseman following him: "Summoning up, therefore, a show of courage, he demanded in stammering accents—'Who are you?'" But the horseman does not reply. Irving leaves this answer to his reader.

Look in any library or book store and you will find editions of *Sleepy Hollow* categorized with children's books, probably by the very same people who lump all cartoons into the category of children's programs. This is unfortunate because *Sleepy Hollow* is *not* a children's story. Irving is a challenging read on three counts: his writing style, his vocabulary, and finally, the historical time-frame from which he wrote (including those customs and ideas outside a modern reader's frame of reference). Combined, these factors create a barrier for many readers to fully appreciate *The Legend of Sleepy Hollow*.

The Lexile Framework for Reading is a numeric value used to measure an individual's reading level or the difficulty of a text. The Lexile tool is useful because it helps connect readers to texts that they can read successfully. The Lexile rating for *Sleepy Hollow* is 1,440, which is higher than Hawthorne's *The Scarlet Letter* (1,400L), and substantially higher than Newbery Award Winners *Maniac Magee* (Jerry Spinelli, 820L), *Holes* (Louis Sachar, 660L), and *The Whipping Boy* (Sid Fleischman, 570L). In fact, a reader with a Lexile of 660 could be expected to comprehend just 8% of *The Legend of Sleepy Hollow* (according to the Lexile Calculator available at Lexile.com).

Of that 8%, what is it the child gets out of this children's story? *The Headless Horseman.* Nothing else sticks. Not Ichabod, not Brom Bones, and certainly not their rivalry for the hand of Katrina Van Tassel. Is it any wonder that *The Legend of Sleepy Hollow* is synonymous with the Headless Horseman?

There are two uncertainties in *The Legend of Sleepy Hollow*: Was the Headless Horseman really a ghost or was it just Brom Bones? Did Ichabod Crane die or live?

Many people assume that answering the first set of alternatives determines the answer to the second, but actually the questions are mutually exclusive. Look:

Scenario One: The Headless Horseman is a ghost who kills (or spirits) Ichabod Crane away from Sleepy Hollow.

Scenario Two: The Headless Horseman is a ghost who scares Ichabod Crane away from Sleepy Hollow.

Scenario Three: Brom Bones, in the guise of the Headless Horseman, kills Ichabod Crane.

Scenario Four: Brom Bones, in the guise of the Headless Horseman, scares Ichabod Crane away from Sleepy Hollow.

Many readers only see scenarios one and four as options, failing to recognize that the ghost may also have scared Crane into leaving the area as surely as Bones could have; or that Bones could have killed Crane as surely as the ghost may have.

None of the story-tellers of this legend, from its original anonymous teller at the corporation meeting to Diedrich Knickerbocker to Geoffrey Crayon or Washington Irving, provide conclusions for the reader to decide which of the above scenarios is the "true" resolution of the story. Instead, the reader is left with this responsibility, interpreting clues or hints from the telling. It is because Irving left Crane's fate unresolved, let his reader make judgments for him or herself, and allowed the shadow of the Headless Horseman to sway these judgments that *The Legend of Sleepy Hollow* has remained an American masterpiece for nearly two hundred years.

Andrew Winkel

ANDREW WINKEL

lives in Clifton, Illinois, with his wife, Milissa, and four children, Alex, Bryan, Katherine, and Anna. He is a 1996 graduate of Columbia College Chicago's Fiction Writing Program, and in 2001 he earned his M.A. from Olivet Nazarene University. He has taught middle school in Bradley, Illinois, since 2001, and has also been the director of the Clifton Public Library since 2006. He is the author of *Raceboy and Super Qwok Adventures*, also published by Hierophantasm. Follow him at andrewwinkel.com.

WASHINGTON IRVING

was born in New York in 1783, studied law and was admitted to the bar of New York in 1806. While conducting business in London he wrote *The Sketchbook of Geoffrey Crayon, Gent.*, which contained *The Legend of Sleepy Hollow* and *Rip Van Winkle*. He died near Tarrytown, New York, in 1859 as one of America's most celebrated and well-known authors. During the 1890s a bust of Irving was placed alongside eight other great men in the front entrance to the Library of Congress in Washington, D.C., as a lasting tribute to his importance to American literature.

THE DISAPPEARANCE OF ICHABOD CRANE

Cover and interior book design: Andrew Winkel

Cover image: Andrew Winkel

Set in OFL Sorts Mill Goudy Regular and Italic, designed by Barry Schwartz, www.crudfactory.com

With dingbats from Nymphette, designed by Lauren Thompson, www.nymphont.com, and footnote numbers from Linux Libertine, linuxlibertine.org

Additional fonts used in the design of this book include:

League Gothic (www.theleagueofmoveabletype.com)

Goudy Bookletter 1911, also designed by Barry Schwartz

Cabin, designed by Pablo Impallari (www.impallari.com) and Igino Marini (www.ikern.com)